Rising From the Ashes

The Hope Series, Volume 2

Colton Lee

Published by Colton Lee, 2024.

Prologue: Resurgam

The world didn't crumble overnight. It fractured, piece by piece, with every storm that tore through the skies and every ember that fell to the earth. Cities burned, forests withered, and seas swallowed lands whole. When it was over, what remained was unrecognizable—a shell of the world Emmalyn had once known.

She stood at the edge of the scorched valley, her fiery hair tangled and wild from the winds that never ceased to howl across the barren plains. In her hands was a blade that hummed with latent energy, its etched runes glowing faintly under the twilight sky. Her left arm, sleek and mechanical, bore the weight of her past and the promise of her future.

The arm had not been her choice, but it had become a part of her. Constructed of reinforced alloys and etched with faint glowing lines of arcane circuitry, it moved as naturally as her original arm once had. And yet, it could never replace what was lost. It whirred softly as she flexed her fingers, a stark reminder of the price she had paid during the Burning Year—the year she had learned how easily the world could burn, how quickly the old life could vanish in smoke and flame.

At first, the arm had felt like a burden, as foreign as the ruins of the cities that now dotted the landscape. But over time, she had come to see it as something more. It was strength forged from pain, resilience born from destruction. Now, as she stood on the precipice of the future, she saw it as a symbol—a reminder that even from ruin, something new could rise.

"Are you sure this is the place?" a voice asked from behind her.

Emmalyn turned to face her sister, Annabeth, whose calm and steady presence had been her anchor through the chaos. Clad in gleaming armor that seemed almost alive with energy, Annabeth embodied the stories of the heroes they'd grown up hearing about. But Emmalyn knew better. Beneath the armor was the same girl who had once fretted over every decision, who had dreamed of something more beyond their sleepy village of Eldridge.

"It's the place," Emmalyn replied, her voice firm despite the doubt gnawing at the edges of her resolve. "If we're going to start again, it has to be here."

Annabeth's gaze dropped briefly to the mechanical arm before returning to her sister's face. Her expression was thoughtful, and Emmalyn could almost hear the words her sister was holding back.

"It's fine," Emmalyn said quickly, lifting the blade in her metal hand. "Stronger than before, remember? Better. So don't give me that look."

"I wasn't giving you a look," Annabeth replied, a faint smile playing on her lips.

"Sure, you weren't," Emmalyn said, turning back to the valley with a smirk.

The sun dipped below the horizon, casting the land in shades of crimson and gold. For a brief moment, the world seemed to hold its breath, the silence stretching endlessly.

Then, like a whisper carried on the wind, the valley came alive with light. Embers rose from the earth, swirling together in intricate patterns, as though the land itself were responding to their presence.

"Resurgam," Emmalyn murmured, the word unfamiliar on her tongue yet carrying a weight she couldn't ignore.

Annabeth tilted her head. "What does that mean?"

"I shall rise again," Emmalyn said, her voice quiet but firm. "That's what this is—what we are."

"Resurgam," Annabeth echoed, her hazel eyes bright with determination.

Together, the sisters stepped into the valley, ready to rebuild a world that had been broken but not destroyed.

The Light of the Path

The ruins of Eldranth sprawled across the horizon, jagged remnants of a world long forgotten. Emmalyn adjusted the strap of her pack, the whirring of her mechanical arm a quiet counterpoint to the soft hum of the blade at her side. Her fiery hair, streaked with ash and dirt, clung to her sweat-dampened forehead as she squinted into the distance.

Beside her, Annabeth knelt near a crumbled column, her gloved fingers brushing away the dust from an engraved stone. Her armor shimmered faintly, its soft light casting intricate shadows across the ancient script.

"Anything?" Emmalyn asked, her voice cutting through the oppressive stillness.

Annabeth studied the inscription, her hazel eyes narrowing. "'And you shall be called the repairer of the breach, the restorer of streets to dwell in,'" she recited softly, reading from Isaiah 58:12. Her voice carried a weight that made the verse feel as much a command as a promise.

Emmalyn frowned. "I'm guessing that's supposed to be encouraging. But unless that stone's going to magically patch up this mess, I don't see how it helps."

Annabeth's lips quirked into a faint smile. "It's not about fixing this place," she said, gesturing to the crumbled ruins around them. "It's about fixing us."

Emmalyn sighed, resting her metal hand on the hilt of her sword. "I really hope whatever we're here for is worth it."

Annabeth stood, brushing dust from her knees, and pointed toward a collapsed archway. "There's something beneath that rubble. I can feel it."

Of course there is, Emmalyn thought, suppressing the urge to roll her eyes. She strode toward the debris, her mechanical arm flexing as she began shifting chunks of stone with practiced efficiency. The servos hummed softly, the glow from her arm illuminating the dust-filled air.

Annabeth joined her, their movements synchronized as they worked to clear the path. Beneath the rubble, a faint glimmer of light began to emerge, pulsing softly in the dim twilight.

"What is that?" Emmalyn asked, squinting at the source.

Annabeth didn't answer immediately. She reached out and carefully pulled away the last fragment of stone, revealing a gleaming object—a golden lamp, shaped like a chalice with delicate, flame-shaped designs carved into its surface.

"It's an oil lamp," Annabeth said, her voice tinged with awe.

Emmalyn tilted her head, skepticism etched across her face. "An oil lamp? That's what we've been digging for?"

Annabeth knelt beside the artifact, her fingers hovering over its intricate carvings. "It's more than that," she murmured. "Look."

The lamp's carvings glowed faintly as Annabeth touched it, their light spreading outward in a slow ripple. Inscribed around its base was a verse: *The spirit of man is the lamp of the Lord, searching all his innermost parts.*

"That's Proverbs 20:27," Annabeth said, her voice hushed.

Emmalyn leaned closer, her mechanical arm's faint glow reflecting off the lamp's surface. "It's beautiful," she admitted reluctantly. "But what does it do?"

As if in response, the lamp flared to life, casting a brilliant golden light that filled the chamber. The carvings on the walls lit up, revealing scenes of battle, rebuilding, and renewal. At the center of it all was the lamp, held aloft by a figure clad in radiant armor.

Annabeth's breath caught. "It's a guide," she said. "A lamp to light the path forward."

Before Emmalyn could reply, a low rumble echoed through the ruins. Shadows began to coalesce in the corners of the room, their forms twisting and shifting.

Emmalyn gripped her sword, her mechanical fingers tightening around the hilt. "Of course. It wouldn't be a treasure hunt without company."

The shadows surged forward, their shapes indistinct but menacing. Annabeth stood, the lamp held firmly in her hands, its light flaring as the creatures approached. The golden glow pushed them back, but they regrouped, circling the sisters with renewed determination.

"Stay behind me," Emmalyn ordered, stepping forward. Her sword flared to life, its runes glowing in response to the lamp's light.

Annabeth nodded, holding the lamp high. The golden light seemed to pulse in time with her heartbeat, growing brighter as the shadows pressed closer.

The first creature lunged, and Emmalyn met it with a swift strike of her blade. The runes on the sword flared, cutting through the shadow as if it were made of smoke. The creature dissolved with a piercing shriek, but more took its place.

Annabeth closed her eyes, whispering a prayer. "*The Lord is my light and my salvation; whom shall I fear?*" The lamp flared brilliantly, sending a wave of light across the room. The shadows faltered, their forms flickering under its brilliance.

Emmalyn pressed the advantage, her blade flashing as she struck down the remaining creatures. The lamp's light grew steadier, its warmth filling the chamber as the last of the shadows dissipated.

Breathing heavily, Emmalyn lowered her sword and turned to Annabeth. "Well, that was fun. Is this thing always going to come with a fight?"

Annabeth smiled faintly, her hands still cradling the lamp. "Probably. But the lamp will guide us."

Emmalyn sheathed her blade and let out a long breath. "Fine. Let's hope it guides us somewhere less deadly next time."

The sisters stood together, the lamp's light casting phoenixes and flames onto the walls around them. The air felt lighter now, filled with quiet purpose.

The path ahead was still uncertain, but with the lamp as their guide, they would not falter.

A Light in the Dark

The light from the golden lamp guided their steps as the sisters made their way through the crumbling ruins of Eldranth, its glow flickering like a beacon in the deepening twilight. The air felt different now, lighter—freer. The shadows that had threatened to swallow them moments ago had receded, but Annabeth knew that their journey had only just begun.

As they traversed the ruins, Emmalyn's mechanical arm hummed quietly, her steps measured. Her usual bravado had dimmed, replaced by a quiet intensity that reflected her thoughts. The lamp in Annabeth's hands continued to shine bright, but there was still an unease in the air, as though something—or someone—was watching them.

"You're awfully quiet, Em," Annabeth remarked, glancing at her sister.

"Just thinking," Emmalyn muttered, her gaze scanning the shadows around them. "You really think this lamp is the key to all of this?"

"I do," Annabeth said with certainty. "It's leading us to something—someone, maybe."

The ruins stretched out before them, empty and silent, save for the distant whistle of the wind. A breeze swept through the desolate streets, lifting dust and old parchment from the ground. The sun had completely set now, leaving only the soft glow from their lamp to light the way.

"Hold up," Emmalyn said suddenly, stopping in her tracks. "Do you hear that?"

Annabeth strained her ears, listening. At first, there was nothing—just the wind and the whispering of the ruins. But then, in the distance, a faint sound reached them: the slow, rhythmic click of wheels on stone.

"Wheels?" Emmalyn said, her voice laced with disbelief.

Before Annabeth could answer, a figure emerged from the darkness ahead. A tall man, his silhouette outlined by the faint glow of their lamp, rolled toward them slowly but steadily. He was in a wheelchair, his posture straight and unyielding, his gaze sharp. Despite the wheelchair, there was no mistaking the presence of a warrior in him. His dark leather armor, worn but well cared for, spoke of battle and survival. A long sword rested on his lap, the blade etched with symbols of protection, and a crossbow was slung across his back.

He stopped a few feet from them, the wheels of his chair grinding to a halt with a soft squeak. His face was angular, with a quiet intensity, and his brown eyes held both wisdom and wariness.

"You're the ones," the man said, his voice deep and calm. "I've been expecting you."

Annabeth blinked in surprise, taking a cautious step forward. "Who are you?"

The man smiled, a flicker of something almost like amusement in his eyes. "Name's Josh. But people call me 'Wheels.'" He extended a hand, his grip firm despite the chair. "I'm here to help you."

Emmalyn arched an eyebrow. "Help us? With what, exactly?"

Wheels chuckled softly, his expression never wavering. "I know the path you're on. I've walked it myself."

Annabeth studied him, her curiosity piqued. "You know about the lamp?"

"Know about it?" Wheels leaned forward slightly, his chair creaking with the motion. "I've seen it. And I've seen what happens when it leads the right people to the right place." He glanced at Emmalyn's mechanical arm, his gaze thoughtful. "You've both been chosen, whether you realize it or not. This lamp? It's not just a symbol. It's a key to something far bigger."

Annabeth's fingers tightened around the lamp, and for a moment, the light flared brightly, casting a warm glow over Wheels. "How do you know all of this?" she asked.

He smiled again, his eyes reflecting a depth of understanding. "Because I've walked this path before. And I've learned that we're all called to rise from the ashes—one way or another." His eyes turned toward Emmalyn's arm. "I see you've already had a taste of what that means."

Emmalyn scowled, though there was no malice in her eyes. "What's your story, then?"

Wheels' expression softened slightly, though there was no hint of regret in his voice. "I was once like you. I fought in the wars that burned this world to the ground. Lost my legs to a landmine, but I didn't lose my will. I've kept moving, even when it seemed like there was no reason to." He looked at Annabeth, then back at Emmalyn. "I've been where you are—looking for purpose in a broken world. The difference is, I've had time to figure out where it leads."

Emmalyn didn't say anything at first, but after a moment, she gave him a hard look. "You sound like you've got all the answers. But this world's a mess, and it doesn't take a genius to know that. What makes you think you can help us?"

Wheels' eyes twinkled, as if he'd expected this. "Because sometimes, the right people find each other at the right time. And when they do, they're capable of things they never imagined. You'll see." He turned his chair slowly, his wheels clicking with purpose. "I know the way. And it's not just about surviving anymore. It's about what we rebuild, together."

Annabeth exchanged a glance with Emmalyn, uncertainty still lingering in the air. But something in Wheels' demeanor—his confidence, his calm—struck a chord with her.

"Alright," Emmalyn said with a shrug, though there was a hint of curiosity in her tone. "Show us the way, then. But if this turns out to be some wild goose chase—"

"You'll get more than you bargained for," Wheels interrupted with a smile that was both knowing and kind.

Emmalyn didn't argue. With a sharp nod, she stepped forward, her mechanical arm gleaming in the dim light. Annabeth followed closely behind, the golden lamp still glowing softly in her grasp.

Wheels led them through the desolate streets, his chair gliding effortlessly over the uneven ground. As they walked, he shared what he knew—stories of the old world, of the battles fought, and of the glimmers of hope that had survived the destruction.

"This place—this land—it's not beyond redemption," he said quietly. "But only if we can rise from the ashes, just like the phoenixes in the carvings. Only if we choose to believe that something good can come from all this destruction."

Emmalyn and Annabeth listened, both moved by the quiet strength of the man before them. They had both lost so much, but there was something in Wheels' words that ignited a spark—a sense that they were on the edge of something bigger than themselves.

As the trio moved deeper into the ruins, the golden lamp continued to glow brighter, its light cutting through the darkness like a promise. They weren't alone anymore. And for the first time in a long while, they weren't just surviving.

They were starting to rise.

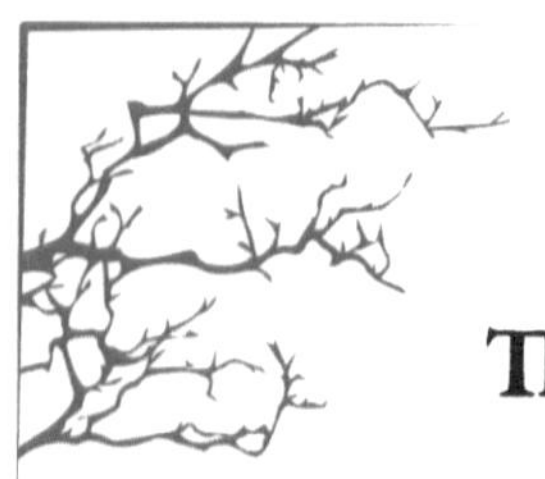

The Road Behind

The night had settled over the ruins, the faint light from their lamp casting long shadows on the crumbling streets. The wind howled in the distance, but here in the broken remnants of Eldranth, the world felt still, as if holding its breath.

Wheels led the sisters through the deserted streets, his chair gliding effortlessly over the uneven stone. The rhythmic click of his wheels was a steady presence, marking the silence that had taken hold of the world. Despite the heavy atmosphere, there was a sense of purpose in his movements, as if every turn, every pause, was guided by something deeper.

"Why here?" Emmalyn asked, breaking the silence. "Why did you come to this place? Seems a little... abandoned for a guide."

Wheels didn't respond immediately. His brown eyes, always keen, scanned the surroundings as if seeing more than the ruins around them. He stopped by a small fountain, its stone basin dry and cracked. For a moment, he seemed lost in thought, his fingers resting lightly on the wheels of his chair.

"I came here because this is where everything changed for me," he said quietly, his voice soft but steady.

Annabeth, sensing the weight of his words, took a step closer. "What happened here?"

Wheels glanced at her, his gaze distant, as if the memories were both familiar and painful. "I wasn't always like this," he began, the weight of his past settling between them. "I wasn't always... sitting." He paused, taking a deep breath before continuing. "I was once a soldier. A warrior, just like you two."

Emmalyn raised an eyebrow. "You? A warrior? You don't exactly look like one of those 'battle-hardened' types."

Wheels chuckled, a low, almost bitter sound. "I suppose not. But I've had my share of battles, fought in the wars that tore this world apart. I was part of the last line of defense in the east. We fought for survival, for the chance to rebuild. But the truth is, there wasn't much left to rebuild by the time we realized it was too late."

The weight of his words settled on the air like a thick fog. Annabeth stayed quiet, sensing that Wheels wasn't just recounting the past for the sake of telling stories.

"I was a commander," he continued, his voice distant. "Leading a small but fierce group of soldiers. We were stationed at a stronghold just outside the southern mountains—cut off from the rest of the world by the storms and the war. We fought to keep the peace, to protect what little was left of the old world. But eventually, we ran out of resources, out of men, and... out of hope."

Emmalyn's eyes softened, her usual sarcasm replaced by curiosity. "What happened?"

Wheels let out a long sigh, his gaze dropping to the dry stone of the fountain. "We were ambushed. It was supposed to be a routine mission. I sent my men to retrieve supplies from a nearby village. But we didn't know it was a trap. By the time I arrived, they were all gone. The village was wiped out, and the ground was scattered with the wreckage of our own soldiers. The trap was meant for us—just a small force that had nothing left to give. But they underestimated us."

He paused, a shadow crossing his face. "I was one of the only ones left alive. But not unharmed. I was hit by a landmine—explosive, powerful. Took my legs. Left me with nothing but the wreckage of a life I couldn't go back to."

Annabeth's heart sank as she listened, but she didn't interrupt. She could see now how the weight of his past shaped him—how the warrior in him had been lost, not to age, but to a world gone mad.

"After that," Wheels continued, his voice steady but tinged with regret, "I was left with two choices: to die on that battlefield, or to live in the ruins of a world I didn't understand anymore. I chose to live." He looked up at them then, his brown eyes reflecting both pain and resilience. "I had to keep moving, even when I couldn't walk anymore. I wasn't sure why at first, but now I know—it wasn't just about survival. It was about finding purpose. About learning that even when everything is lost, you can still choose to rise from the ashes."

Emmalyn and Annabeth exchanged a glance. It was clear that, in his own way, Wheels had walked the same path they were on now—fighting not just for survival, but for something bigger. A sense of purpose.

"So, what happened to the rest of your group?" Annabeth asked, her voice gentle.

Wheels shook his head, his lips pressed into a thin line. "They didn't make it. And neither did the stronghold. The world collapsed around us, faster than we could keep up. By the time I made it to the edge of the ruins, there was nothing left but empty roads and the ashes of the past."

He paused, the weight of the years pressing down on him. "But I didn't give up. I found people—survivors—just like you. I learned that, sometimes, it's not about being strong enough to save the world. It's about being willing to stand up and try, even when it feels like everything is stacked against you."

Emmalyn was quiet for a moment, processing his words. The skepticism that usually colored her tone was absent now, replaced by something like understanding.

"So, you came here because you think we're part of the answer?" she asked, her voice softer than usual.

Wheels gave a small nod, his expression resolute. "I don't know if you're the answer. But I believe you're part of the journey. And the lamp you carry?" He looked at Annabeth, his gaze piercing. "It's more than just a guide. It's a sign that you're on the right path. The world needs people who will rebuild it, not just fight for scraps. You two are those people."

Annabeth felt a stirring in her chest. The words were simple, but they were profound in a way that made her feel something she hadn't allowed herself to feel in a long time: hope.

"Alright," Emmalyn said, breaking the silence. "You've got my attention. Let's see if this 'rebuild the world' thing actually works out. But if this path leads us straight into some more monsters or broken cities, I'm holding you personally responsible."

Wheels chuckled, his expression softening. "Fair enough. But remember, it's not about the monsters or the cities. It's about what we do with the pieces we have left. And together, we've got a lot more than we think."

The three of them stood there for a moment, the weight of their shared purpose settling between them. In the distance, the faintest glimmer of dawn began to break on the horizon, casting a pale light over the ruins.

The world was still broken. But as long as they had the will to move forward, it wasn't beyond repair.

The Ties That Bind

The morning light filtered weakly through the remnants of the ruined city, casting pale beams across the desolate streets. The air was still, heavy with the weight of a world long forgotten. The golden lamp that Annabeth carried now felt even more significant, its glow a beacon of something that could still be saved in this broken world.

Wheels rolled quietly ahead, the steady click of his chair on the cracked pavement echoing in the silence. The sisters, following close behind, could sense that today was different. There was an undercurrent of anticipation in the air, something unspoken that neither Annabeth nor Emmalyn could fully place. Wheels had been their guide for days now, but today, it felt like they were approaching something more—something bigger than just survival.

As they rounded a corner, the sound of distant voices drifted toward them, rising above the eerie quiet of the ruins. The group paused, and Wheels gave a small nod, signaling for them to be quiet. They followed him down a narrow, overgrown alleyway, their steps cautious.

At the end of the alley, a small, makeshift camp was set up—tents constructed from tarps and remnants of old buildings, and a fire burning low at the center. A handful of people moved about, gathering supplies and tending to the fire. Most were young, their faces drawn with the hard lines of survival, but there was a sense of community here—a shared bond in the midst of all the chaos.

Wheels wheeled forward, his chair moving smoothly over the cracked ground. One of the survivors, a woman with short, dark hair, spotted him and straightened. She was wearing a vest adorned with various symbols of their survival—a stark contrast to the broken city around them.

"Wheels!" she called, a smile lighting her face as she jogged over to him. "You made it back."

Wheels' face softened at the sight of her. "Kelli," he said, his voice warm. "We're all in one piece. I brought some company."

The woman, Kelli, looked past him and noticed Annabeth and Emmalyn. Her smile grew, though there was a cautious curiosity in her gaze. "I see that," she said, glancing at the sisters. "New blood, huh? I'm Kelli." She extended her hand to Annabeth first, then Emmalyn. "You've got a long road ahead of you, I can tell."

Annabeth shook her hand, smiling politely, though her eyes lingered on the camp, sensing that this group was different. There was a quiet strength here, something they hadn't seen much of since leaving the safety of their village.

Wheels gave a small nod. "They're with me," he said simply. "They've got a purpose. A light to follow."

Kelli's expression softened. "We could use more of that around here," she said, turning toward the campfire. "Come. You're welcome to stay for a while. We've got food, and some shelter for the night."

The sisters exchanged a look, silently agreeing. They had traveled far, and there was no sense in pushing forward without understanding more about the people who had found their way here.

As they walked toward the camp, the woman with short hair moved aside to let them pass. Several others paused from their tasks to watch, their eyes flicking between the newcomers and the man in the wheelchair. One of the survivors—a young man—walked up to Wheels, a grin spreading across his face.

"Dad!" the young man exclaimed, and the joy in his voice was unmistakable. He was tall, with shaggy brown hair and an easy smile that made him look years younger than the world around them. "I was starting to think you wouldn't make it back. Got worried when you didn't come by last night."

Wheels smiled at his son, his eyes softening at the sight of him. "Noah, you know me. I don't stay down for long."

Noah reached down to help his father with a steadying hand, careful as he adjusted the wheels of the chair. "Yeah, but you're not getting any younger, old man," he teased, though there was a deep respect in his voice.

Kelli shook her head, smiling as she made her way over to a small firepit. "Don't encourage him," she said, her tone affectionate. "If I didn't know better, I'd say Noah was the one keeping the camp alive."

The young man laughed, clearly used to the lighthearted teasing. "Maybe. But don't worry, Mom. I'm not going anywhere."

Annabeth and Emmalyn exchanged glances, both taking in the dynamic between the three. There was something deeply comforting about the way Kelli and Noah interacted with each other, and the way Wheels seemed to light up when he saw his son. Despite the harshness of their world, here, in this small corner of the ruins, was a family—one that had survived by holding together.

"Thanks for the welcome," Emmalyn said, breaking the silence. "We could use a break. And we're still figuring out what comes next."

Kelli smiled warmly. "You're in the right place for that. We've all been trying to figure out what comes next. But we've learned that we can't do it alone. Together is the only way forward."

Emmalyn nodded, a faint smile crossing her lips. For the first time in a while, she felt like maybe, just maybe, they weren't the only ones struggling to find meaning in the chaos.

"We've been trying to rebuild, too," Annabeth said, stepping forward. "It's not just about surviving anymore. It's about finding a way to move forward."

Kelli's gaze softened, and she gestured toward the campfire. "That's what we've been doing here. Surviving's easy when you're just trying to make it through another day. Rebuilding—that's the hard part. But we've got something a little different, something that's been keeping us going. You've probably seen it already."

The lamp, still glowing in Annabeth's hands, seemed to flicker in response. She held it out, its warm light casting long shadows. "This? It's guiding us. But we don't know exactly what it's leading to."

Kelli looked at the lamp and nodded thoughtfully. "It's a symbol of hope. Something we haven't had much of, but something we can't afford to lose." She met Annabeth's gaze with understanding. "We've all seen what happens when you let the darkness take over. But we're here, aren't we? We're still fighting."

As the conversation continued, Emmalyn's attention turned to Noah, who had wandered over to speak with the other survivors. He was speaking to an older man with a weathered face, showing him something that looked like a map—perhaps a plan for the next stretch of their journey.

"Your son's a good guy," Emmalyn said, her voice quiet. "He's got the kind of fire that'll help him survive."

Wheels nodded, his brown eyes softening with pride. "Noah's been my reason for pushing forward. He's strong—stronger than he realizes. Kelli and I raised him right. He'll be part of whatever comes next."

"I'm not sure what that is yet," Emmalyn muttered, looking up at the sky. "But I'm starting to think it might not be as bad as we thought."

Wheels turned his chair toward her, his voice steady but filled with the weight of hard-earned wisdom. "It never is. Not when you've got people to share the journey with."

The warmth from the campfire flickered around them, casting shadows that stretched long and far, but in that moment, amidst the ruins, there was something more—hope, something that had been in short supply for so long. And for the first time, it didn't feel impossible to believe they might actually be able to rebuild.

They didn't have all the answers. But they had each other. And that might just be enough.

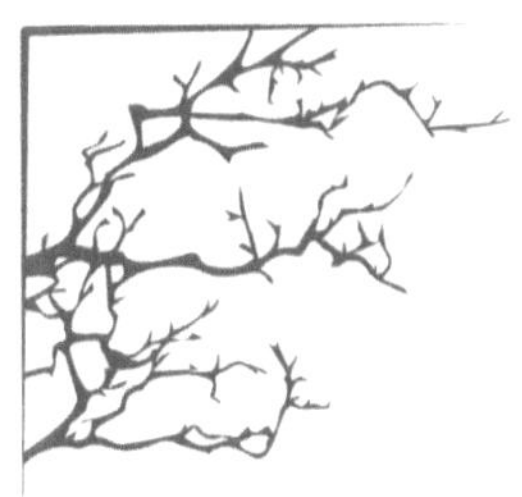

The Darkness
Approaches

The morning air in the camp was cool, with a light mist hanging over the ruins. The golden lamp that Annabeth carried, still glowing softly, illuminated the faces of the survivors as they moved through their daily routines. There was a fragile peace in the air, a brief calm that hinted at the strength they had managed to cultivate in a world that had long since forgotten what peace felt like.

Emmalyn was sharpening her blade near the fire, the rhythmic scrape of steel on stone a comforting sound amid the quiet bustle. She looked up at Noah, who was speaking to his mother, Kelli, near one of the makeshift tents. The weight of their journey had yet to take its toll on him—his face was still youthful, his energy unwavering. But Emmalyn saw the way his eyes held a glimmer of something deeper, something that mirrored his father's strength.

Wheels, his gaze always alert, sat nearby. His brown eyes scanned the surroundings, sensing the shift in the air before anyone else could. He had a way of knowing when something was wrong, an instinct shaped by years of survival in a world where danger was always just out of sight.

"Stay alert," Wheels murmured, his voice low and steady. "There's something in the wind."

Annabeth, who had been adjusting the lamp's glow, stiffened. "What do you mean?"

"Something's off," Wheels replied, his voice steady. "Can't quite place it, but stay ready."

Emmalyn felt it too—a growing tension in the air, a quiet before the storm. The mist around them seemed thicker, darker, and the usual sounds of wildlife or distant movement had disappeared. It felt as though the world was holding its breath.

Suddenly, a sound broke through the silence—a deep, guttural growl that reverberated in the air. Then came the screeching, high-pitched and eerie, a noise that made the hairs on the back of Emmalyn's neck stand on end. The ground beneath them seemed to shift, the vibrations unmistakable.

"Get to the fire!" Kelli shouted, her voice filled with urgency. "Now!"

Chaos erupted as the survivors rushed to arm themselves, grabbing what weapons they had. Emmalyn's hand went to her sword instinctively, her mechanical arm flexing as she prepared for what was coming.

"Noah! Stay close," Wheels commanded, his voice calm but firm. He gripped the arms of his wheelchair with determination, moving toward the center of the camp.

The first of them appeared—shadowy figures, moving with unnatural speed and coordination. Their eyes glowed a fiery red, burning through the mist, and their forms were humanoid but twisted—flesh corrupted and grotesque, their bodies contorted in unnatural ways. They were demons—beasts from beyond the veil, creatures of the darkness sent to destroy whatever light remained in this broken world.

"Demons," Emmalyn muttered, her voice filled with disbelief. She had heard stories, but she never imagined she would face them herself.

Wheels didn't hesitate. "Everyone form a defense! Do not let them get close!"

Annabeth stood beside Emmalyn, gripping her blade. "We've got to fight them off. Keep them from the fire!"

The demons let out a spine-chilling howl as they charged. Emmalyn met them head-on, her blade cutting through the air with practiced precision. Her mechanical arm swung with unnatural strength, cutting down the first demon that came at her. The creature screeched as it collapsed, its twisted body writhing before going still.

But there were more. Many more. The demons poured from the mist like a flood, their eyes burning with malice as they surged toward the camp. Each one was larger than a man, with claws that could tear through flesh, and eyes that burned with an insatiable hunger.

"Stay together!" Kelli shouted, swinging a heavy axe as she joined the fray. "We can do this!"

Emmalyn's sword cleaved through another demon's chest, but she could feel the weight of their numbers pressing in. There were too many of them, and the survivors were spread too thin. She could see Noah, fighting fiercely with a spear, but even he seemed overwhelmed by the onslaught.

"Annabeth!" Emmalyn shouted, backing up to her sister. "We need to take down their leader. If we don't, this won't end!"

Annabeth, her eyes filled with resolve, raised the golden lamp high. Its light flared brighter, cutting through the shadows and illuminating the chaos around them. "We go for the one controlling them," she said, her voice firm.

In the distance, through the shifting haze, a larger figure stood out—a towering demon, its form imposing and regal, its eyes burning with a malevolent intelligence. It stood at the back of the pack, watching the battle unfold with cold detachment.

"That's the one," Annabeth said, her eyes narrowing. "If we can take it down, the others will scatter."

The sisters pushed through the battle, cutting down demons that got too close. Emmalyn's sword and mechanical arm moved with lethal grace, each strike felling a demon before it could reach the survivors.

The air was thick with the acrid scent of smoke and blood, the sound of battle ringing in her ears.

When they finally reached the leader, the massive demon let out a growl of fury. Its eyes locked onto them with a predatory gaze, and it swung a massive claw toward Annabeth. She barely managed to block the strike with her sword, the force of the blow sending her stumbling back.

Emmalyn stepped forward, her sword raised high. "Get back!" she shouted to Annabeth, her voice harsh and urgent.

With a swift motion, she lunged forward, her blade cutting deep into the demon's side. The creature howled, rearing back, but it wasn't enough to take it down. It swung at her with terrifying speed, its claws narrowly missing her.

"Annabeth, now!" Emmalyn shouted.

Annabeth raised the lamp higher, its glow burning brighter than ever. The demon recoiled, its glowing eyes flickering. The light from the lamp seemed to intensify, filling the air with a sense of power, as if it was calling on something far beyond their understanding.

With a final, desperate strike, Emmalyn plunged her sword deep into the demon's chest. It howled in rage and agony as its body shuddered, then collapsed to the ground with a heavy thud.

The remaining demons hesitated, their leader dead. For a moment, the battle seemed to pause. Then, with a shriek of fury, they began to retreat, their bodies dissolving into the mist from which they had come.

The camp fell silent. The battle was over, but the survivors were left panting, their bodies covered in sweat and blood. The demons were gone, for now, but the tension in the air remained.

Emmalyn lowered her sword, wiping the blood from its edge. "That was too close."

Annabeth, her hand still gripping the lamp, nodded. "We can't afford to be caught off guard like that again."

Wheels, his face grim but steady, turned to Noah. "Get the camp secured. We'll need to move soon."

Noah nodded, his face drawn with the weight of the fight. "Understood, Dad."

Kelli walked over to the sisters, her eyes tired but full of gratitude. "Thank you. We wouldn't have made it without you."

Emmalyn gave a small nod. "It's what we do."

Wheels watched the mist slowly clear, his brown eyes narrowed. "This won't be the last time they come," he said quietly. "The demons are hunting us. And they won't stop until we're all gone."

Annabeth tightened her grip on the lamp, its golden light flickering. "Then we keep fighting," she said firmly. "We'll rebuild, no matter how many times they tear us down."

The survivors gathered around the campfire, exhausted but determined. They had won this battle, but the war was far from over. And the light from the lamp, faint as it may be, would guide them through the darkness ahead.

The End of the Beginning

The camp was quiet now, the fire crackling softly as the last embers of the battle faded into the night. The demons, their twisted forms now nothing more than fading echoes in the wind, had retreated, leaving behind the aftermath of their brutal assault. The survivors were gathered around the fire, tending to their wounds, their faces marked with exhaustion and relief. The golden lamp still glowed softly in Annabeth's hands, its light flickering in the growing darkness.

Emmalyn sat apart from the group, her sword resting beside her as she cleaned the blood from her mechanical arm. The tension from the fight still lingered in the air, but there was something more now—a quiet sense of realization that weighed heavily on her. She glanced up at the stars, knowing that somewhere beyond them, the world had already started to crumble.

Wheels sat nearby, his wheelchair positioned close to the fire, his brown eyes scanning the group as he listened to the murmurs of conversation. He had always been a man of few words, but tonight, the silence between them felt different. It felt like the calm before the storm, as if the real battle was only just beginning.

Kelli approached, sitting beside him and resting her hand briefly on his shoulder. Noah was helping the younger survivors, making sure everyone had what they needed. The camp was in good hands, but there was still a heaviness that lingered, a weight that even the most resilient among them couldn't shake.

Wheels cleared his throat, breaking the quiet. "I know we've just come out of one hell of a fight," he said, his voice low but steady. "But

I need to tell you all something. Something you've probably already figured out for yourselves."

Annabeth, her brow furrowing, leaned in a little closer, sensing the shift in the air. Emmalyn looked up, her expression unreadable. The camp seemed to hold its breath as they all turned toward him.

"We've been in the end times for a while now," Wheels continued, his voice firm, though there was an undercurrent of grief. "The world's been dying for years. And those demons... they're not just random monsters. They're part of something bigger. Something we've been warned about for a long time."

Annabeth's eyes narrowed, but she remained quiet, listening intently. Emmalyn leaned forward, her heart beginning to race as she sensed the gravity of his words.

"The signs are all around us," Wheels said, his eyes distant, as if seeing something beyond the campfire's glow. "The wars. The storms. The chaos. It's all part of God's prophecy. We're living through the end, the final days before Christ returns. The demons—the fallen ones—they've been sent to usher in the darkness. They're here to destroy everything, to take as many souls as they can before it's all over."

Annabeth's breath caught, and Emmalyn felt a chill run down her spine. She had suspected something was wrong with the world, but hearing it from Wheels—hearing it confirmed—felt different. It was one thing to live through the aftermath of a broken world. It was another to realize that everything they had been fighting for, all the years of survival, had been leading to this moment.

"But why us? Why this?" Annabeth asked, her voice trembling slightly. "We're just... survivors. How are we supposed to stop this?"

Wheels let out a slow breath. "We're not supposed to stop it, Annabeth. We're supposed to bring people to Christ. We're meant to be vessels for His light in this darkness. Our mission, no matter how impossible it seems, is to lead people to the truth of the gospel before it's too late. To share Christ's love, His grace, and His salvation—because in the end, that's the only thing that will save anyone."

Emmalyn's chest tightened, the weight of his words sinking deep into her. Her mind raced—was this what they were really doing? Not just surviving, but fighting for something far greater than they had ever imagined?

She looked at Wheels, seeing the strength in his eyes, the man who had already walked through so much darkness and still held on to faith. She saw something else too—a hope that had burned in him despite everything. He had been through the worst of it, and yet, here he was, still standing, still guiding them toward something beyond the chaos.

"And the lamp?" Annabeth asked quietly, glancing at the golden light in her hands. "What does this have to do with it?"

Wheels' gaze shifted to the lamp, and for a moment, his expression softened. "The lamp is a symbol," he said, his voice thick with meaning. "It represents the light of Christ, the only true light that can drive out the darkness. We're not just holding it. We're supposed to share it—spread that light, show others the way. That's our mission. And right now, in this broken world, that's our only hope."

Emmalyn was quiet, processing his words, her heart heavy with the weight of it all. She had always been a fighter, someone who relied on her strength, her blade, her resolve. But now, she felt something new stirring within her. A calling. A purpose beyond just surviving.

"You think there's still time for that?" Emmalyn asked, her voice hoarse. "For people to turn back? For anyone to hear us?"

Wheels met her gaze, and for the first time, she saw the full depth of his belief. "There's always time for those who choose to hear," he said quietly. "Christ's grace is infinite. The demons may think they've won, but they haven't. There's still time. And as long as we're here, as long as we're breathing, it's our job to keep the light burning."

Annabeth nodded slowly, her grip tightening around the lamp. She could feel its warmth, its power—a promise that there was still a chance, even in the darkest of times.

"We're not alone," she said softly. "We have this light. We have each other. And we have Christ."

Wheels' face softened, his eyes filled with a quiet gratitude. "That's right. We're a family, and we have a purpose. We'll keep fighting, even when it seems impossible. Because the light... the light will lead us through."

The camp fell silent as everyone reflected on his words. The fire crackled softly, and the lamp's golden glow continued to burn brightly, casting long shadows on the faces around it. For the first time in a long while, Emmalyn felt something beyond the weight of survival. She felt the weight of their mission—something bigger, something that could bring salvation even in the darkest hour.

The demons might have been driven back for now. But the true battle was just beginning. And as long as the light burned, they would not face it alone.

The Ghosts of the Past

The morning sun filtered weakly through the clouds as the group packed up the camp, its light casting long shadows on the barren landscape. The aftermath of the battle with the demons still hung in the air, but there was no time to dwell on it. They had a mission, and they couldn't afford to rest for long. With the golden lamp still glowing faintly in Annabeth's hands, they set out again, unsure of what awaited them, but certain of their purpose: to bring the light to those who still needed it, to guide them to something greater.

Wheels led the way, his eyes scanning the horizon. His calm presence was a steady anchor, a silent reminder of the mission at hand. Emmalyn walked beside him, her mind occupied with thoughts of the previous night. She hadn't spoken much since the attack, but the events were still fresh in her mind—especially the chilling presence of the demons, the reminder that they were always just a step behind.

Noah, strong and unwavering, helped organize the survivors as they moved out. Kelli, too, kept her focus, making sure the others were ready for anything.

The land around them was vast and desolate. Fields of tall, dry grass stretched as far as the eye could see, the remnants of small towns scattered along the way, their ruins barely recognizable. No sign of life, just ashes and broken walls.

By midday, the group came across a town, or rather what was left of one. The buildings were reduced to smoldering piles of rubble, the streets littered with the wreckage of what had once been a thriving community. There were no sounds—no signs of movement, just the oppressive quiet of destruction.

Emmalyn was the first to speak. "This place... It's been hit hard. Whoever did this wasn't playing around."

Kelli's voice was low and tense. "No signs of survivors. This wasn't a random attack."

"Looks like a raid," Annabeth said quietly, her eyes scanning the ruins. "But this... this was different. There's no one left."

Wheels rolled forward, his eyes narrowing as he took in the destruction. "The demons hit this place, I'm sure of it. But it doesn't make sense. Why leave it like this? Why let it burn without finishing the job?"

The group ventured deeper into the town, the heavy silence pressing down on them as they navigated the wreckage. The streets were eerily still, the air thick with the smell of smoke and charred wood.

Then, something caught Emmalyn's eye. Amidst the rubble, something—someone—moved. A figure, barely visible, lying still but breathing. She sprinted toward it, her instincts kicking in.

"Over here!" Emmalyn shouted, her voice sharp with urgency.

Annabeth and Kelli quickly followed, rushing toward the figure buried beneath debris. As they cleared the rubble, their eyes widened in recognition.

"It's Colt," Annabeth whispered, her heart skipping a beat.

Emmalyn froze. "Colt? From our last adventure on the mountain?" she asked, disbelief coloring her voice.

Annabeth nodded, her eyes filled with concern. "It's him. He's alive."

They gently lifted Colt's battered form, laying him carefully on the ground. His clothes were torn, his face bloodied and bruised. He was breathing, though faintly, and his eyes flickered open for a brief moment, full of confusion.

"Colt, hey," Annabeth said softly, leaning closer. "Can you hear me? It's Annabeth."

His eyes met hers, clouded and distant. "Annabeth... Emmalyn..." He coughed weakly. "I... thought I'd lost you both..."

"Not yet," Emmalyn said with a grin, despite the gravity of the situation. "But you're in bad shape. You need help."

"Was... wasn't ready for this..." Colt muttered, his voice barely audible. "Wasn't ready for any of it..."

Annabeth knelt beside him, her hand on his shoulder. "We're going to get you out of here, Colt. Just hang in there."

Wheels, who had rolled closer to the group, let out a low sigh as he studied Colt. His brown eyes softened as he gazed at the man lying before them, and Emmalyn could see the weight of the past in his expression.

"You know him?" Kelli asked, her voice tinged with curiosity.

Wheels nodded, his gaze still locked on Colt. "Yeah, I know him. We fought together back in the wars. We were a team—a darn good one too."

Annabeth's eyes widened. "You fought together? I didn't know you two were—"

"Yeah," Wheels interrupted, his voice quieter now. "We fought side by side. But after everything fell apart, Colt... he disappeared. He went his own way. I lost track of him after that." He sighed deeply, the pain of old memories resurfacing in his tone. "It's been a long time."

Emmalyn stood up, her mind racing. "What happened to him? Why did he end up here, like this?"

Wheels' gaze remained fixed on Colt, who was now unconscious again, his face pale. "We fought for survival. That's all we ever did. But after the wars, after everything fell apart... I think Colt lost something. He didn't just lose his body, he lost his will to keep fighting. I think he was looking for something more—something to believe in. But whatever he's been through since... it's taken its toll."

Kelli moved closer to Wheels, her voice softer now. "None of us are the same as we were before. The world's been changing too fast."

"Exactly," Wheels said, his eyes still on Colt. "We lost everything. But some of us found a reason to keep going. Others..." He trailed off, his voice heavy with regret.

Annabeth turned to look at Colt, her heart aching for the man who had once helped them survive a deadly journey on the mountain. He had been strong, a fighter. But now he looked fragile—broken by a world that seemed to have chewed him up and spit him out.

"We can't just leave him here," Annabeth said firmly, her voice full of determination. "We'll take him with us. He's been through hell, but we'll help him. We'll make sure he gets the chance to fight again."

Emmalyn nodded. "I agree. Let's get him back to the camp. He needs medical attention, and we can't let him die here, not after everything he's done for us."

Wheels gave a small nod, the faintest hint of approval in his eyes. "Alright, let's move. But we'll need to be careful. If demons were here, they might come back. We can't afford to stay in one place for too long."

Noah approached them, his face a mask of concern. "What happened here? How did this place fall?"

Wheels looked around at the ruined town, his eyes scanning the wreckage. "I don't know. But this isn't just some random attack. Whoever did this knows what they're doing. And they're not done."

Emmalyn's hand tightened on her sword. "We'll be ready. Let's get out of here before more demons show up."

With Colt carefully carried between them, the group began to make their way out of the destroyed town. As they moved, the wind picked up, carrying with it a faint echo of distant cries, as though the town itself was mourning the lives lost here.

The world was falling apart. But with every step they took, they carried the light with them. And as long as they had each other, as long as the lamp burned bright, they would keep fighting—not just for survival, but for a future, for a reason to keep going when everything seemed lost.

Together, they would rebuild. And with every soul they saved, they would bring the light one step closer to driving back the darkness.

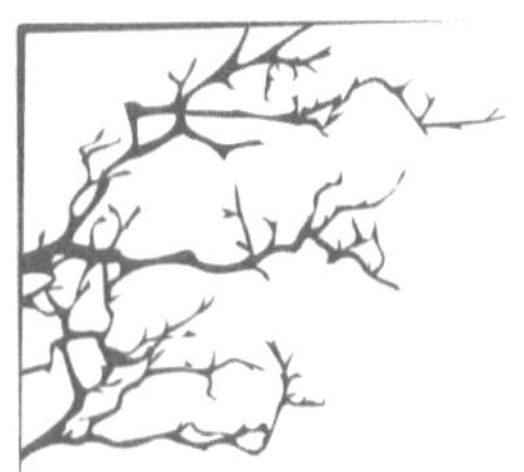

Broken Chains

The group moved quickly, leaving the ruined town behind as the sun dipped lower in the sky. The dry wind carried the faint smell of smoke, but there were no immediate signs of pursuit. Still, Wheels urged them onward. The demons had left their mark on the town, and he knew they would return—if not to this place, then somewhere else, hunting for the living.

Colt's unconscious form was draped across a makeshift stretcher carried by Noah and Emmalyn, their pace steady but urgent. Kelli walked beside them, her sharp eyes scanning the horizon for any threats. Annabeth kept close to Wheels, the golden lamp in her hands glowing softly as though it could sense their purpose.

They reached a sheltered grove near the edge of a forest just as night began to fall. The survivors quickly set up camp, keeping their voices low and their movements careful. They couldn't afford to draw attention. The light from the lamp was enough to keep the area around them visible without giving away their position.

As the others worked, Annabeth knelt beside Colt, checking his injuries. His breathing was steadier now, though his face was pale and his body battered. She wiped away the dirt and blood from his forehead, her brow furrowing with concern.

"He's stronger than he looks," Wheels said from behind her, his voice quiet. He had rolled his chair closer, his eyes fixed on Colt's face. "Always has been."

Annabeth glanced up at him, her expression thoughtful. "You know him better than we ever did. He saved Emmalyn and me on that mountain—led us out when we were surrounded. He didn't have to, but he stayed. I never forgot that."

Wheels gave a small nod, his face heavy with memory. "That sounds like Colt. Always throwing himself into the fire for someone else." He paused, his gaze distant. "He wasn't always like this, you know. Before the wars, he was the best soldier I'd ever fought beside. Smart, fearless, loyal to a fault. But when the world fell apart, he took it harder than most. He wanted to save everyone. When he couldn't, it broke him."

Annabeth sat back, letting the weight of his words sink in. "Do you think he'll come back from this?"

Wheels studied Colt for a long moment before speaking. "He's been carrying chains for a long time—guilt, regret, anger. But chains can be broken. I think that's why we found him. He's still got a part to play."

As if on cue, Colt stirred, his head rolling slightly to one side. His eyes fluttered open, unfocused at first, but slowly sharpening as they landed on Annabeth's face.

"Annabeth?" His voice was hoarse, barely more than a whisper.

She smiled, relief washing over her. "Yeah, it's me. You're safe now."

He coughed weakly, his voice gaining a little strength. "Didn't... think I'd see you again."

"You weren't making it easy," Emmalyn said from nearby, her tone wry. She stepped closer, crossing her arms. "What were you doing in that town, Colt? Looked like you were trying to take on the whole mess yourself."

Colt gave a faint, humorless chuckle. "Not exactly. Was tracking a group of survivors. Heard they were in trouble. Got there too late." His eyes darkened, the weight of his failure clear.

Annabeth reached out, resting a hand on his shoulder. "You're here now. That's what matters."

Colt shook his head, his jaw tightening. "Does it? I've been running for so long, trying to make up for all the times I wasn't fast enough. It's never enough."

Wheels leaned forward slightly, his voice steady but firm. "It's not about what you've done, Colt. It's about what you do next. You've still got time to make things right—not by fixing the past, but by choosing a different future."

Colt's eyes flicked to Wheels, recognition sparking in his gaze. "Wheels? I thought... I thought you didn't make it after the last raid."

Wheels gave a small smile, his voice warm. "Takes more than a few demons to keep me down." He hesitated, then added, "We're on a mission, Colt. To bring people to Christ. To guide them out of the darkness before it's too late. And we could use someone like you."

Colt let out a shaky breath, his expression conflicted. "You think there's still time? For anyone?"

"There's always time," Wheels said firmly. "As long as you're breathing, you've got a chance. And so does everyone else we're trying to save."

The camp fell quiet, the weight of the conversation settling over them. The fire crackled softly, and the golden lamp continued to glow, its light casting warm shadows across their faces.

Finally, Colt nodded, his voice steady despite the emotion in it. "Alright. If you think I can still do some good... I'm in. I owe you that much."

Annabeth smiled, her heart lightened by his words. "You don't owe us anything, Colt. We're in this together."

Emmalyn stepped forward, her expression softening. "Welcome to the team, then. Just try not to get yourself killed this time."

Colt managed a weak chuckle, his first real smile breaking through. "No promises."

The group settled in for the night, their spirits lifted despite the dangers that still surrounded them. Colt's presence felt like a victory, a reminder that even in the darkest times, there was still hope.

As the stars emerged above the grove, Wheels looked up, his brown eyes reflecting the faint glow of the lamp. He whispered a quiet prayer, thanking God for the light that continued to guide them.

They were still broken, still scarred, but they were together. And with every step forward, they were one step closer to fulfilling their mission.

The end was coming. But so was redemption.

The Gathering of the Lost

The sun rose over the forest as the group broke camp and began their journey again. The air was cool, with the promise of a long day ahead. The golden lamp glowed softly in Annabeth's hands, its light steady and warm, a symbol of the mission they were beginning to fully embrace.

The landscape around them was stark and quiet, but there was a feeling of urgency in the air, a sense that the time to act was now. Wheels led the group, his sharp eyes scanning the horizon as they made their way through the desolate countryside. Colt walked beside him, his steps steadier now, though his face still bore the weariness of someone who had seen too much.

"We'll find them," Wheels said quietly, sensing Colt's inner turmoil.

Colt glanced at him, his expression skeptical. "And when we do? What if they don't want to listen? What if they've given up?"

Wheels' voice was calm but firm. "That's not our decision to make. All we can do is share the truth. The rest is up to them—and to God."

The group pressed on, moving through the ruins of a once-thriving farming community. Fields that had once been lush and green were now overgrown with weeds, the barns and houses reduced to skeletons of their former selves.

Then, faintly, they heard it—a muffled cry, carried on the wind. Annabeth stopped, her heart pounding. "Did you hear that?"

Noah nodded, his hand tightening on the spear he carried. "It's coming from over there." He pointed toward a collapsed barn in the distance.

Without hesitation, they moved toward the sound, their pace quickening as the cries grew louder. When they reached the barn, they found a small group of people huddled together, their faces pale and drawn. They looked up in fear as the group approached, their eyes wide and desperate.

"It's okay," Annabeth said gently, holding up her hands. "We're here to help."

One of the survivors, a woman with short-cropped hair and a wary expression, stepped forward. She held a makeshift weapon in her hands, her posture defensive. "Who are you? What do you want?"

"We're just travelers," Wheels said, his voice calm and steady. "We've been where you are, and we know what it's like to lose everything. We're not here to hurt you."

The woman's eyes flicked to the lamp in Annabeth's hands, the golden glow reflecting in her wary gaze. "What's that?"

Annabeth stepped forward, her voice quiet but full of conviction. "It's a light—a reminder that there's still hope, even in a world like this. We're here to share that hope with you, if you'll let us."

The woman hesitated, glancing back at the others in her group. There were five of them, all looking just as lost and afraid as she did. Finally, she lowered her weapon. "We've been running for days," she said, her voice breaking. "The demons... they destroyed everything. We don't know where to go."

Wheels rolled closer, his brown eyes filled with compassion. "You're not alone anymore," he said. "We can help you, but there's something you need to know. The world is in its final days. The things you've seen—the destruction, the chaos—it's all part of what was foretold. But there's still time to find peace. To find salvation."

The survivors exchanged uncertain glances, their fear mingling with curiosity. One of them, a young man with a bandaged arm, spoke up. "Salvation? What are you talking about?"

Annabeth took a deep breath, holding the lamp higher. "We're talking about Christ. About the one who offers hope and light in the darkest times. He's the only one who can save us now—not just from the demons, but from the darkness inside us. All we have to do is turn to Him."

The group was silent for a moment, the weight of Annabeth's words hanging in the air. The woman who had spoken first looked at Wheels, her voice trembling. "Why would He save us? After everything we've done, after all the things we've lost... why would He care?"

Wheels' expression softened, and his voice was steady as he replied. "Because His love doesn't depend on what we've done or what we've lost. It's not about earning it. It's a gift, freely given. All you have to do is accept it."

The young man with the bandaged arm looked down, his jaw tightening. "You make it sound so simple. But I've seen too much... done too much... to believe that."

Emmalyn stepped forward, her voice firm but gentle. "We've all seen things, done things we wish we could take back. You're not alone in that. But it's not about being perfect—it's about trusting that His grace is bigger than anything you've done. He's not asking for perfection. He's asking for your heart."

The group was quiet again, their faces reflecting the battle waging within them. Finally, the woman spoke. "If this... if He's real, and if there's still time, then... what do we do?"

Wheels smiled faintly, his voice filled with quiet conviction. "You pray. You ask Him into your heart. You ask for forgiveness and trust Him to guide you. And you let His light lead you out of the darkness."

Annabeth knelt beside the woman, her hand resting lightly on her shoulder. "We can help you. You don't have to do this alone."

The woman hesitated, tears welling in her eyes. Then, slowly, she nodded. "Okay," she whispered. "Okay."

One by one, the survivors followed her lead, their heads bowing as they prayed. It was a simple prayer, but it was enough—a first step toward the light, toward a hope they hadn't believed was possible.

As the last prayer was spoken, the golden lamp flared briefly, its light glowing brighter for a moment before settling back into its steady warmth. The group looked at it in awe, their fear giving way to something new—something that felt like peace.

"You're not alone anymore," Annabeth said, her voice soft but certain. "We'll walk this path together."

The survivors gathered their few belongings, their faces showing a mix of relief and determination. They weren't the same people they had been moments ago. Something had changed, and for the first time in a long while, they had hope.

As the group continued their journey, the lamp's light guided them forward, a beacon in the darkness. For every soul they found, every heart they guided, the mission became clearer: they were the light-bearers, the ones called to lead the lost to salvation.

The world was falling apart, but as long as they carried the light, they would keep moving forward, bringing hope to those who needed it most.

The Weight of the Sheepdog

The day's journey had been long, the landscape a patchwork of ruined farms and crumbled roads. The golden lamp still glowed in Annabeth's hands, its light casting a faint warmth as the group settled into a clearing to rest. The newly found survivors huddled together, still uncertain despite their earlier prayers. Fear lingered in their eyes, the trauma of their losses fresh and raw.

Colt sat by the fire, his shoulders hunched as he sharpened his knife. His movements were steady, but his gaze was distant, lost in memories he didn't want to relive. Across from him, Wheels adjusted his position, his sharp brown eyes observing the survivors and their unease.

"You're thinking too hard," Wheels said finally, his voice calm but firm.

Colt glanced up, a humorless smile tugging at his lips. "Can't help it. This world doesn't leave much room for peace of mind."

Wheels leaned forward slightly, his elbows resting on the arms of his chair. "That's because you're still carrying too much weight. You can't fix the past, Colt. You know that."

Colt's grip tightened on the knife. "Doesn't mean I stop trying. Someone has to do something. Someone has to protect the ones who can't fight back."

Wheels nodded slowly, his expression thoughtful. "You ever hear about the sheepdog?"

Colt frowned. "The what?"

"The sheepdog," Wheels said. "It's an old idea. There are three kinds of people in this world. The sheep, who can't defend themselves; the wolves, who prey on the weak; and the sheepdog, who protects the flock." He paused, his voice growing softer. "The sheepdog doesn't fight for glory or revenge. He fights because it's in his nature to protect. It's who he is."

Colt stared at him, the words settling heavily in the space between them. "So, what are you saying? That I'm supposed to be a sheepdog? That I'm supposed to save everyone?"

Wheels shook his head. "You can't save everyone, Colt. But you can save someone. You can fight for those who can't fight for themselves. That's what it means to be a protector. Not just with your hands, but with your heart."

Colt looked down at the knife in his hand, the weight of Wheels' words sinking in. He had spent so long fighting, running, trying to make up for the lives he couldn't save. But maybe it wasn't about saving everyone. Maybe it was about standing up for the ones who still had a chance.

Before he could respond, Emmalyn approached, her expression tense. "We've got a problem."

Wheels straightened. "What kind of problem?"

"The new survivors," Emmalyn said, her voice low. "They're whispering. Eyeing the rest of us like we're the enemy."

Colt's hand went to his knife instinctively. "What are they planning?"

"I don't know," Emmalyn admitted, glancing over her shoulder. "But they don't trust us. They're scared. And scared people do reckless things."

As if on cue, a shout rang out. The group spun toward the source, their weapons ready. The new survivors had armed themselves with makeshift weapons—clubs, pipes, and knives—and were advancing toward them, their faces hard with fear and suspicion.

"You've been lying to us!" the woman with short hair shouted, stepping forward. Her voice trembled, but her grip on the pipe she carried was steady. "That light of yours—it's not natural. You're leading us into a trap!"

Annabeth stepped forward, holding the lamp high. "It's not a trap. This light—it's from God. It's here to guide us, to protect us."

"You expect us to believe that?" another man spat, his face twisted with anger. "We've seen what the demons can do. How do we know you're not working with them?"

"We're not your enemy," Wheels said, his voice calm but firm. "We've been where you are—lost, afraid. But you need to trust us. We're here to help."

But the fear in the survivors' eyes had turned to something darker—desperation. They advanced, their weapons raised, and the clearing erupted into chaos.

Emmalyn and Colt moved quickly, stepping between the group and the rest of their allies. Emmalyn's sword gleamed as she blocked a swing from one of the attackers, her mechanical arm catching the pipe and twisting it out of their grasp. Colt fought with precision, disarming another survivor without harming them.

But in the confusion, Annabeth was pulled back. A pair of the survivors, moving with practiced speed, grabbed her, dragging her away from the group.

"Annabeth!" Emmalyn shouted, her eyes widening as she saw her sister being taken.

Annabeth struggled, but the attackers were strong. They disappeared into the woods, leaving the rest of the group behind.

"Enough!" Colt growled, stepping forward. His knife glinted in the firelight as he barked, "Stand down! This isn't a fight you can win."

The remaining survivors hesitated, their fear beginning to crumble under the weight of Colt's words. Slowly, they lowered their weapons, their expressions shifting to confusion and shame.

Emmalyn didn't waste a moment. "Noah, Kelli—stay here and secure the camp. Colt, Wheels, you're with me. We're getting Annabeth back."

Wheels nodded, his voice steady. "Let's move."

The three of them set off into the woods, the golden light from the lamp fading in the distance. Annabeth's absence was a weight on all of them, but there was no room for doubt. They would find her.

Because that's what sheepdogs did. They protected the flock, no matter the cost.

Lost in the Shadows

The dense forest stretched endlessly before them, the canopy above blotting out much of the moonlight. Emmalyn's boots crunched against the underbrush as she moved quickly, her mechanical arm gripping her sword tightly. Colt followed close behind, his steps quieter but no less purposeful, while Wheels maneuvered through the uneven terrain with practiced skill.

The urgency in their search was palpable. Annabeth's absence left a void in their group, her light and calm resolve now replaced by a gnawing sense of desperation.

"She couldn't have gotten far," Emmalyn said, her voice strained as she pushed through the brush. "We just need to pick up the trail."

Colt knelt near the edge of a shallow creek bed, scanning the ground. The soil was disturbed, footprints visible in the mud. "They crossed here," he said, pointing to the tracks. "But it's messy—too many to tell which way they went after this."

Wheels rolled to a stop beside him, his sharp brown eyes narrowing as he scanned the surrounding woods. "They're covering their tracks," he said, his tone grim. "Whoever took Annabeth, they know what they're doing."

Emmalyn's frustration boiled over, and she slammed her sword into the ground, the blade sinking deep into the soft soil. "We can't lose her! She's out there, with strangers who don't trust us, and we're just... stumbling around!"

Colt stood, his expression calm but firm. "Getting angry won't help us find her, Emmalyn."

"Then what will?" she snapped, turning to him. "Because so far, all we've done is waste time."

"Enough," Wheels said, his voice cutting through the tension. He adjusted his position, his chair steady on the uneven ground. "We'll find her. But not like this."

Colt nodded. "Wheels is right. We need to think. These people are scared, desperate. They won't hurt her—not unless they think they have no other choice."

Emmalyn's jaw tightened, but she said nothing. She knew Colt was right, but the thought of her sister in danger was unbearable. Annabeth had always been the heart of their group, the one who carried the light—not just the lamp, but the hope they all clung to. Losing her, even temporarily, felt like losing part of herself.

Wheels turned his gaze back to the ground, studying the faint footprints. "We follow this path until we lose it completely. If it goes cold, we regroup and think of another plan. But we don't give up."

With a reluctant nod, Emmalyn retrieved her sword and the group pressed on. The trail led them deeper into the forest, the footprints becoming harder to distinguish as the ground grew rockier. The air was thick with tension, every snap of a twig or rustle of leaves putting them on edge.

After what felt like hours, they came to a clearing where the trail abruptly ended. Colt knelt again, running his fingers over the dirt. "It's gone," he said quietly, frustration evident in his voice.

Emmalyn let out a growl of frustration, pacing the edge of the clearing. "This can't be it. They didn't just vanish."

"They might have doubled back," Wheels said, his voice steady. "Or taken to the trees. Either way, they've outmaneuvered us for now."

Colt stood, his expression grim. "We need to head back to camp. If we keep going blind, we'll exhaust ourselves—and we can't protect anyone if we're worn out."

Emmalyn's fists clenched, but she knew he was right. Still, the idea of leaving without finding Annabeth made her stomach churn. "We can't just... leave her out here," she said quietly.

Wheels rolled up beside her, his voice softer now. "We're not leaving her, Emmalyn. We're regrouping. That's what a sheepdog does. We don't rush in and make things worse. We plan, and we fight smart."

She swallowed hard, nodding reluctantly. "Fine. But we're coming back out here as soon as we can."

The three of them turned back toward camp, the weight of their failure hanging heavily over them. The forest seemed darker now, the absence of Annabeth's light more noticeable with each step.

When they returned to the clearing where the others were waiting, Kelli and Noah rushed to meet them.

"Did you find her?" Kelli asked, her voice hopeful but strained.

Emmalyn shook her head, her shoulders slumping. "We lost the trail."

Noah's face fell, his grip tightening on his spear. "What do we do now?"

"We rest," Wheels said firmly. "We don't do anyone any good if we're too tired to think straight. Tomorrow, we come up with a new plan."

The group settled in for the night, the campfire casting flickering shadows on their faces. Emmalyn sat apart from the others, staring into the flames. Her thoughts were consumed by her sister—where she was, what she was enduring, whether she was safe.

Colt approached, sitting down beside her. He didn't say anything at first, simply letting the silence fill the space between them.

"She's strong," he said finally. "Stronger than you give her credit for. She'll hold on until we find her."

Emmalyn glanced at him, her expression softening slightly. "I just can't stop thinking about what might be happening to her. What if we're too late?"

Colt's voice was steady. "Then we fight to make sure we're not."

Wheels watched the fire from his spot nearby, his thoughts turning to Annabeth and the golden lamp she carried. Its light had been a constant presence, a reminder of their mission. Without it, the camp felt emptier, colder.

He bowed his head, whispering a quiet prayer. "Lord, guide her steps. Protect her in the darkness, and help us to bring her back. We need her light—Your light."

The night pressed on, heavy with unanswered questions and the weight of what lay ahead. They didn't know where Annabeth was, or what she was facing, but they knew one thing for certain: they wouldn't stop searching until she was back where she belonged.

Lessons from the Journal

The camp was quiet in the early morning, the last remnants of the night's chill still lingering in the air. Emmalyn sat near the firepit, staring at the worn leather journal in her hands. Annabeth's journal. Its edges were frayed, the clasp bent slightly, but the pages within held something precious: Annabeth's faith, her guiding light, written in her own careful hand.

The young survivor who had taken it, the woman with the dark braid, sat a short distance away, her posture tense. She hadn't spoken since she returned the journal, her guilt visible in every nervous glance. Emmalyn had wanted to be angry, but holding the journal now, all she felt was a profound sense of loss.

"You're awfully quiet," Wheels said, rolling up beside her. His brown eyes softened as he noticed the journal in her hands. "Thinking about Annabeth?"

Emmalyn nodded, brushing her thumb over the clasp. "She wrote everything in here—Bible verses, prayers, notes about how to keep going. It's like... part of her is here with us. But it's not the same."

Wheels leaned forward slightly, his voice gentle but firm. "She carried this because it reminded her of who she is and what she's fighting for. Maybe it's time you carried it, too. Not just for her, but for them." He gestured toward the new survivors, who were sitting huddled together, their faces still marked with fear and uncertainty.

Emmalyn followed his gaze, her jaw tightening. "They don't trust us. They barely trust themselves. What am I supposed to do with that?"

"Show them," Wheels said simply. "They're scared, just like we've all been. But you've got something they don't—hope. Use that journal. Teach them what Annabeth would have."

Emmalyn looked back at the journal, flipping it open to a familiar page. The verse at the top caught her eye: *"The Lord is my shepherd; I shall not want."*

Taking a deep breath, she stood and walked toward the group of survivors. They tensed as she approached, their gazes wary, but they didn't move away. The woman with the braid—Clara, as Emmalyn had learned—watched her with a mix of guilt and curiosity.

Emmalyn knelt down, holding up the journal. "This belonged to my sister," she began, her voice steady. "She wrote in it every day. Bible verses, prayers, reminders to herself about why she kept going. She called it her anchor."

Clara's brow furrowed. "Why are you telling us this?"

"Because she would have told you," Emmalyn said simply. "She would have shared this with you, just like she shared it with me. She believed that faith isn't something you keep to yourself—it's something you give to others."

The survivors exchanged uncertain glances, but no one interrupted. Emmalyn opened the journal to another page and began to read aloud: *"Even though I walk through the valley of the shadow of death, I will fear no evil, for You are with me; Your rod and Your staff, they comfort me."*

"That's from Psalm 23," she explained. "Annabeth wrote it here because she believed it, even when everything around us was falling apart. She trusted that God was with her, no matter how dark things got."

Clara's voice was soft, almost hesitant. "How could she believe that? After everything that's happened... how could she still trust in God?"

Emmalyn met her gaze, her expression both firm and compassionate. "Because she knew that this world isn't the end of the story. She believed in something bigger than herself—bigger than all of this. And she knew that no matter how much we lose, God's love doesn't change."

The group was quiet for a moment, the weight of her words settling over them. Then, one of the younger survivors, a boy no older than sixteen, spoke up. "Do you... do you think He's with us, too? Even after everything we've done?"

Emmalyn nodded, her voice gentle. "He's with all of us. His grace doesn't depend on what we've done. It's not something we can earn—it's a gift. All we have to do is accept it."

Clara looked down, her hands twisting in her lap. "I've done things... things I'm not proud of. How could He forgive me for that?"

Emmalyn knelt closer, placing a hand on her shoulder. "None of us are perfect. But that's the point. Christ came to save us because we can't save ourselves. He offers forgiveness freely, no matter what we've done. All He asks is that we turn to Him."

Wheels, who had been listening quietly, rolled closer. "Faith isn't about being flawless. It's about trusting that God is bigger than your mistakes. That's what Annabeth believed, and that's what we're here to share."

The survivors sat in silence, the flickering firelight reflecting in their eyes. Emmalyn could see the walls they'd built around themselves beginning to crack, the smallest seeds of hope taking root.

She held up the journal again. "I'm going to keep reading from this. If you want to listen, you're welcome to. If you have questions, ask them. This isn't just Annabeth's anchor—it can be ours, too."

One by one, the survivors nodded, their postures softening. Clara wiped at her eyes, a faint smile breaking through her guilt.

As the group settled in, Emmalyn felt something shift within her. She missed Annabeth fiercely, but sharing her sister's faith—her light—gave her a sense of purpose she hadn't felt before.

They weren't just surviving. They were growing. And for the first time since Annabeth had been taken, Emmalyn felt a glimmer of hope that they would find her—and when they did, they'd bring her home to something stronger than before.

For now, they had a mission: to carry the light forward, to share the hope that had been given to them. And with every verse, every whispered prayer, they took one step closer to fulfilling it.

Lessons from the Past

The fire crackled softly in the center of the camp, its warmth spreading out into the cool evening air. Emmalyn sat cross-legged near the flames, Annabeth's journal resting open on her lap. The new survivors gathered around her, their faces a mix of curiosity and lingering fear. They were still hesitant, still uncertain about their place among the group, but they listened.

Clara sat closest to Emmalyn, her dark braid falling over her shoulder as she leaned forward slightly. The other survivors, including the young boy from earlier, sat in a loose semicircle, their eyes fixed on Emmalyn as though waiting for something they couldn't yet define.

Emmalyn looked down at the journal, flipping through its worn pages until she found the verse she'd been searching for. She glanced up, her voice steady as she began. "You asked me yesterday how God could forgive someone who's done terrible things. How He could love someone like that."

Clara nodded slowly, her expression vulnerable.

"Well," Emmalyn continued, "there's a story about a man named David. You might've heard of him—he's the same David who fought Goliath and won."

The boy, who had been sitting quietly, perked up. "The guy with the sling? Took down the giant with one shot?"

"That's the one," Emmalyn said with a small smile. "David was a hero, chosen by God to be king of Israel. He trusted God, and God helped him do incredible things. But David wasn't perfect—not even close."

Her smile faded as she turned her gaze back to the journal. "David did some terrible things. When he became king, he let his power and pride get the better of him. He took another man's wife, Bathsheba, for himself—and when she became pregnant, he tried to cover it up. When that didn't work, he had her husband, Uriah, sent to the front lines of a battle where he was sure to be killed."

The group was silent, the weight of the story sinking in. Clara's eyes widened. "He did that? And God still forgave him?"

"Yes," Emmalyn said, her voice firm. "But it wasn't automatic. David realized what he had done was wrong, and he repented. He went to God in prayer and begged for forgiveness. Psalm 51 is a prayer David wrote after he was confronted about his sins. In it, he says, *Create in me a clean heart, O God, and renew a right spirit within me.*"

She paused, letting the words settle before continuing. "David didn't just say sorry and move on. He turned back to God completely. He admitted his failures, asked for forgiveness, and committed to living differently. That's what made him a man after God's own heart—not that he was perfect, but that he kept coming back to God, no matter how far he'd fallen."

The young boy spoke again, his voice hesitant. "So... even if you mess up really bad, like David, God will still forgive you?"

Emmalyn met his gaze, her expression gentle. "Yes. If you turn to Him, He will always forgive you. God's grace is bigger than any mistake we could ever make."

Clara leaned forward, her voice trembling. "But what about the people David hurt? What about Bathsheba and Uriah? How can God forgive something like that?"

Emmalyn nodded, her face thoughtful. "That's a fair question. David's actions had consequences. He couldn't undo the hurt he caused, and he had to live with the fallout of his choices. But forgiveness doesn't erase consequences—it means God restores our relationship with Him. And when we're forgiven, we can start to make things right with the people we've hurt."

Wheels, who had been sitting nearby, rolled closer. "It's not about pretending the past didn't happen," he added. "It's about trusting God to bring good out of it, even when it seems impossible."

Clara's brow furrowed, her hands twisting nervously in her lap. "I just... I don't know if I can do that. I don't know if I can ask for forgiveness when I feel like I don't deserve it."

Emmalyn leaned toward her, her voice soft but firm. "None of us deserve it. That's the whole point of grace. It's not about earning God's love—it's about accepting the love He's already given us. David didn't deserve forgiveness, but God gave it to him because David turned his heart back to Him. You can do the same."

The group fell quiet again, the only sound the crackling of the fire. Emmalyn glanced around, watching as the survivors processed her words. She knew it would take time—trusting in something so big, so profound, wasn't easy. But she also knew that seeds were being planted, seeds that might one day grow into faith.

She looked back at the journal and read another verse aloud: *"For I know the plans I have for you, declares the Lord, plans for welfare and not for evil, to give you a future and a hope."*

"That's from Jeremiah 29:11," she explained. "Annabeth wrote it down because she believed it was true for all of us. No matter what we've done, God has a plan for our lives—a plan full of hope, if we're willing to trust Him."

Clara wiped at her eyes, her voice barely above a whisper. "I want to believe that."

Emmalyn reached out, placing a comforting hand on her shoulder. "You don't have to figure it all out right now. Just start by talking to Him. He's listening, even if it doesn't feel like it."

The young boy nodded, his expression thoughtful. "Maybe... maybe I'll try that."

Emmalyn smiled, a small spark of hope lighting her heart. "That's all He asks."

As the night deepened, the survivors lingered near the fire, their questions turning into quiet conversations. Emmalyn stayed with them, answering what she could, sharing more of Annabeth's verses and the stories behind them.

For the first time since Annabeth had been taken, Emmalyn felt like she was honoring her sister's mission. She was sharing the light, guiding the lost, and helping others see the hope that had carried them through so much darkness.

And she knew, deep down, that Annabeth would be proud.

A Fight for the Flock

The chill of the early morning hung heavy over the camp as Emmalyn woke to the faint sound of rustling in the woods. Her mechanical arm twitched instinctively, her grip tightening around the hilt of her sword. She sat up, her senses alert. The forest around them was quiet—too quiet.

Across the campfire, Clara stirred, blinking groggily as she noticed Emmalyn's movements. "What is it?" she whispered.

Emmalyn held a finger to her lips, motioning for silence. Her eyes scanned the shadows beyond the trees, her heartbeat quickening. There was something out there—something wrong.

A low, guttural growl broke the stillness, sending a shiver down her spine.

"Wake everyone," Emmalyn said quietly, her voice firm but calm. "Now."

Clara nodded, scrambling to rouse the others. Within moments, the survivors were on their feet, fear etched on their faces as the growling grew louder.

"What's out there?" one of them whispered, his voice trembling.

"Demons," Emmalyn replied, her tone steady despite the dread rising in her chest. "They've found us."

The group huddled together, their makeshift weapons clutched tightly. Emmalyn positioned herself between them and the forest, her mechanical arm flexing as she raised her sword.

"Stay close to the fire," she instructed, her gaze never leaving the darkened woods. "Do not run. Do not scatter. You stay together, and you stay behind me. Understand?"

They nodded, their fear palpable but contained.

The first demon appeared moments later, its twisted form emerging from the shadows like a nightmare made flesh. Its glowing red eyes locked onto the group, and it let out a bone-chilling screech that echoed through the trees.

Emmalyn didn't wait for it to advance. She charged forward, her sword gleaming in the faint firelight as she slashed at the creature. The blade struck true, cutting through its grotesque body with a sickening squelch. The demon fell, but two more appeared in its place.

"Here we go," she muttered, her grip tightening.

The battle erupted into chaos. The demons surged toward the group, their claws slashing through the air as they moved with terrifying speed. Emmalyn fought with precision, her sword cutting through the darkness as she held the line. Her mechanical arm swung with brutal force, sending one demon crashing into a tree with a sickening crunch.

"Behind you!" Clara shouted.

Emmalyn spun just in time to block a strike from another demon, its claws raking against her arm. She shoved it back, her sword plunging into its chest with a fierce cry.

The survivors, though terrified, held their ground. Clara swung a heavy branch at one of the demons, managing to knock it off balance. Another survivor, the young boy Emmalyn had spoken with the night before, thrust a sharpened stick toward a demon, his hands shaking but his aim true.

"Stay together!" Emmalyn shouted, her voice cutting through the chaos. "Keep the fire at your back!"

More demons poured from the woods, their numbers growing as the group struggled to hold them off. Emmalyn's muscles burned with effort, but she didn't falter. Every swing of her sword was a reminder of what she was fighting for—not just survival, but the people behind her, the flock she had sworn to protect.

One of the demons broke through the line, lunging toward Clara. Emmalyn reacted without thinking, throwing herself between them. The demon's claws raked across her side, but she didn't stop. With a fierce cry, she drove her sword into its chest, the blade glowing faintly as the creature dissolved into ash.

"Are you okay?" Emmalyn asked, her voice breathless.

Clara nodded, tears streaming down her face. "You saved me."

"I told you," Emmalyn said, offering a faint smile despite the pain in her side. "Stay behind me."

The tide of the battle began to shift. The demons, though numerous, were disorganized, their attacks growing more erratic as the survivors held their ground. The fire burned brighter, casting long shadows that seemed to push the creatures back.

Emmalyn pressed forward, her sword cutting through the last of the demons with a final, powerful strike. The forest fell silent once more, the only sounds the survivors' ragged breaths and the crackling of the fire.

"They're gone," Emmalyn said, lowering her sword. She turned to the group, her eyes scanning their faces. "Is everyone okay?"

Clara stepped forward, her voice trembling. "We're okay. Thanks to you."

The young boy, still clutching his sharpened stick, looked at her with awe. "You were amazing," he said. "Like a real warrior."

Emmalyn smiled faintly, though her exhaustion was evident. "I'm just doing what needs to be done."

Wheels rolled closer, his gaze steady and calm. "You protected them, Emmalyn. That's what a sheepdog does."

She nodded, the weight of the battle settling over her. "It's not just about fighting, though," she said quietly. "It's about making sure they know why we're fighting. Why we keep going."

She turned to the group, her voice firm but compassionate. "We can't do this on our own. None of us can. That's why we have to trust in something bigger than ourselves. In God. In His strength, not ours."

Clara wiped at her eyes, nodding. "I think... I think I'm starting to understand."

Emmalyn looked down at Annabeth's journal, her grip tightening. "Good. Because that's what Annabeth would want—for us to fight, but also to believe. To trust that we're not alone."

The survivors gathered closer, their fear replaced by a growing sense of hope. The demons had been defeated, but the battle was far from over.

As the first rays of sunlight broke through the trees, Emmalyn felt a renewed sense of purpose. They would keep moving, keep fighting, and keep spreading the light.

Because that's what it meant to protect the flock. And she would not let them down.

Songs for the Journey

The group had been traveling for hours, the forest giving way to open fields and rolling hills as they made their way through the wilderness. Despite the heavy burden of their mission, there was a sense of camaraderie among the survivors. The fires of last night's battle still smoldered in their minds, but they had come together, united by their shared purpose.

Emmalyn walked at the front of the group, her eyes scanning the horizon for any signs of danger. The weight of Annabeth's journal hung in her pack, a constant reminder of the light they carried—one that was both guiding them and anchoring them.

As they walked, Emmalyn couldn't help but hum softly to herself. The songs from her childhood, the hymns Annabeth had once sung, rose unbidden from her heart. It had been so long since she had allowed herself to sing. In the chaos of the world, in the grief and pain, she'd forgotten how much music had once meant to her.

But now, with the group moving forward, she needed it. And, perhaps, they needed it too.

She cleared her throat softly and began to sing, her voice steady and quiet at first.

"Amazing grace, how sweet the sound,
That saved a wretch like me.
I once was lost, but now am found,
Was blind, but now I see."

The survivors, at first startled by the sudden song, gradually slowed their steps and listened. The sound of her voice, though simple, carried a quiet strength—a reminder that even in the darkest of times, there was grace.

Clara, who had been walking close behind, murmured, "That's beautiful."

Emmalyn smiled, her voice growing a little stronger as the wind picked up, carrying the notes through the trees. She didn't care if anyone joined her. Singing these words, these familiar hymns, felt like a lifeline, a way to steady her soul.

After a moment, Clara, then the young boy who had spoken with Emmalyn before, joined in softly. Soon, the rest of the group followed, the melody of *"Amazing Grace"* echoing through the hills. The simple song—so familiar, yet so profound—lifted their spirits in ways words alone could not.

When the song ended, a sense of quiet peace settled over them, as if the very act of singing had bound them together in a way that words alone hadn't.

"That was... nice," the young boy said, his voice shy but sincere.

Emmalyn nodded. "It's an old hymn. One Annabeth used to sing when we were traveling. It reminded her that no matter what we've done, no matter how far we've fallen, grace is always there to lift us."

"Can you teach us some more?" Clara asked, her voice full of hope.

Emmalyn smiled. "Of course."

As the day wore on, Emmalyn began singing more hymns. She taught them *"It Is Well with My Soul,"* her voice rising and falling with the gentle rhythm of the road. *"It is well, it is well, with my soul."* The words seemed to resonate with the survivors, their voices tentative at first, but growing stronger with each verse.

And then, without missing a beat, she led them into *"How Great Thou Art,"* the words flowing with ease as the group joined her in song. Their voices, though rough and uncertain, blended together in a harmony that transcended the hardships they had faced.

"Then sings my soul, my Savior God, to Thee,

How great Thou art, how great Thou art!"

The wind picked up, rustling through the trees as they sang, carrying the sound of their voices across the open fields. For a brief moment, it felt as if time had slowed down—no demons, no battles, no uncertainties. Just the music, the unity, and the grace that flowed from their song.

As the last note faded into the evening air, Emmalyn paused, letting the silence wash over them. The weight of the journey still hung heavy, but somehow, it felt a little lighter now. The hymns, simple as they were, had brought them together. And in that unity, Emmalyn found a small, flickering hope.

She turned to the group, her voice quiet but filled with conviction. "Remember, no matter where we go, we carry His light. And as long as we have faith, we're never truly alone."

The survivors nodded, their faces more at ease than before. They had found something amidst the chaos—a moment of peace, a shared understanding, and the beginnings of a new faith that could carry them through the darkness ahead.

As the sun dipped below the horizon, casting long shadows across the land, Emmalyn felt a renewed sense of purpose. The journey would be long, and there would be more battles to face, but for now, there was music. And in that music, they had found a deeper connection—a reminder of the light they carried, and the strength they drew from each other and from God.

And so, they sang, step by step, through the wilderness, their voices rising with each hymn—a chorus of hope and faith, steady as the road ahead.

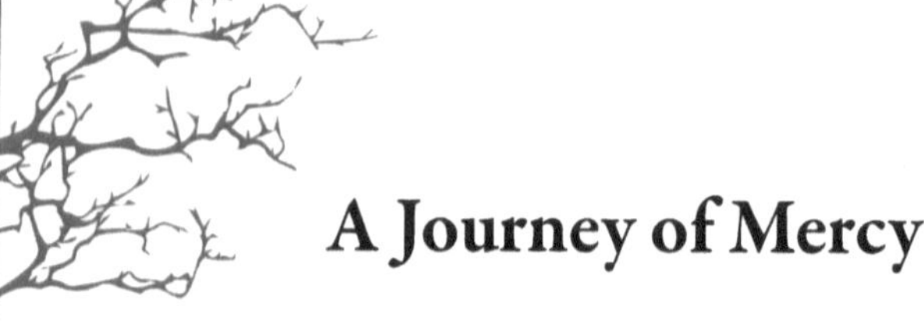

A Journey of Mercy

The days had blurred together as the group continued their journey, moving through desolate landscapes and towns ravaged by destruction. The firelight flickered in the quiet of the evening, casting long shadows across the survivors as they made their camp for the night. Despite the weight of their mission and the fear they carried for Annabeth's safety, Emmalyn could sense something new rising among them—something more than survival: mercy.

Though Noah and his small group were out searching for Annabeth, the rest of the survivors moved steadily through the barren land, helping those they encountered, sharing the little they had left, and spreading God's mercy wherever they could. The trail of the lost was long, but Emmalyn felt as if each small act of kindness was one step closer to bringing the world back to something resembling hope.

The first town they came across was little more than a ghostly shell—abandoned houses with broken windows, empty streets covered in debris. The air was thick with the smell of decay, and the silence was deafening. There were no signs of life.

Emmalyn led the group cautiously through the streets, her senses sharp as she searched for any signs of survivors. It wasn't until they reached the center of town that they saw movement—a figure stumbling from behind a crumbling building. It was a man, his face gaunt from hunger, his clothes torn and stained.

He stopped short when he saw them, his eyes wide with suspicion. "Who are you?" he rasped, his voice hoarse.

"We're not here to hurt you," Emmalyn said gently, holding out her hands in a gesture of peace. "We're here to help. Do you need food or water?"

The man blinked, his expression a mix of disbelief and confusion. "Food?" he asked, his voice trembling. "You've got food?"

"We've got enough to share," Emmalyn said, motioning for Kelli to bring forward a sack of provisions. "You're not alone in this. There are more of us, and we're here to help."

The man staggered forward, as if he couldn't quite believe it, and sank to his knees when the food was placed in front of him. He clutched it to his chest, his hands shaking. "Thank you. I thought... I thought everyone was gone. I've been alone for days."

"You're not alone," Emmalyn said softly, kneeling beside him. "God has always had a way of bringing people together, even in the darkest of times."

The man's eyes filled with tears, and he looked up at her, a flicker of hope in his gaze. "I thought I was the last one left."

"No," Emmalyn said, a small smile touching her lips. "There's still mercy in this world. We're still here."

They spent the rest of the day helping him. They gave him food, water, and blankets to keep warm. Emmalyn shared Annabeth's journal with him, reading aloud from the verses that spoke of hope and trust in God. By the end of the afternoon, the man had regained some of his strength, and though he still had scars of the past, his eyes held a spark of life once more.

As they prepared to leave, he stood shakily and looked at them. "I'll never forget this. You saved me, when I thought there was no one left to care."

Emmalyn placed a hand on his shoulder. "God hasn't forgotten you. And neither have we."

The next town was different. It was small but still populated, though many of the buildings were boarded up, the streets empty except for a few figures moving about cautiously. The survivors stayed close together as they walked down the main street, their eyes scanning for any signs of life.

They approached a woman sitting by the door of a small house, her back against the wooden frame. She looked up as they approached, her expression guarded but not hostile. Her face was drawn, worn with worry, but there was a quiet strength in her gaze.

"We're not here to take anything from you," Emmalyn said, offering her a soft smile. "We've got food and water. We can share what we have."

The woman eyed them for a long moment, then stood, her face softening slightly. "You're the first people I've seen in days. There's not much left, but... we've been holding on."

"We understand," Emmalyn said. "We've all been holding on."

Clara stepped forward, holding out a sack of grain and dried meat. "Take what you need. There's no catch. We're just trying to help."

The woman's eyes flickered with hesitation, but she reached for the sack and began to inspect the contents. "I don't know how you're all still going after everything that's happened," she said quietly. "Most people would've just given up."

Emmalyn's expression softened. "It's not about giving up. It's about trusting that there's something more than this—that we're all part of a bigger story. God hasn't forgotten any of us, even when it feels like the world is ending."

The woman looked down at the food in her hands, then back up at Emmalyn. "I used to go to church... before everything fell apart. But I stopped believing. I couldn't understand why God would let this happen."

Emmalyn nodded. "I get it. I've asked the same questions. But the one thing I've learned through all of this is that God's love doesn't change, no matter how much the world does. We might not have all the answers, but we know that we're not alone in this."

The woman wiped a tear from her eye and looked at the sack of food. "Maybe I've been wrong to turn my back on Him. Maybe it's time to try again."

Emmalyn smiled, feeling the weight of her words settle into the woman's heart. "It's never too late to start over. God's mercy is always waiting for us."

As they moved through the town, offering what food and aid they could, Emmalyn saw the shift in the people's faces—something that had been lost for so long was beginning to take root again. Hope. Mercy. A future.

By the time the sun dipped below the horizon, the survivors had made a difference in two towns. They had offered food, shared stories, and spread the message of God's mercy, one person at a time. They hadn't just survived—they had lived, shown compassion, and given something invaluable to the people they met: a reminder that mercy still existed, even in the darkest times.

As they set up camp that evening, Emmalyn stood by the fire, gazing into the flames. Her heart was full, though the road ahead was still long. The fight for Annabeth continued, but in the midst of it all, the light of God's mercy was shining brighter.

And in that light, she found the strength to keep going, knowing that they weren't alone. Not in this world, and not in the next.

The Return of a Warrior

The fire flickered low in the center of the camp, the survivors gathered around, their faces drawn from the long days of travel. The journey had become a quiet rhythm—a search for Annabeth, a fight for survival, and moments of mercy and kindness along the way. They had settled into the routine of their new life, but the weight of missing their sister and friend lingered heavily on their hearts.

Emmalyn sat near the fire, her eyes scanning the horizon, as if willing Annabeth's return to come soon. She had tried to keep her mind occupied with the work of helping others, but the ache of missing her sister never fully went away.

She heard it first—a faint rustling in the distance, a quiet noise that carried through the night air. She turned, her heart leaping in her chest.

Then, she saw him.

"Noah?" Emmalyn's voice broke through the night air, barely above a whisper.

The figure that emerged from the trees was unmistakable, though he looked different—weathered, worn down, and somehow both stronger and more broken than before. He was walking slowly, using a staff for support. A patch covered his left eye, and his right arm hung loosely by his side. The sleeve of his shirt was torn, and where his hand had once been, there was only a stump wrapped in cloth.

"Noah!" Emmalyn cried, standing abruptly and rushing toward him.

Noah stopped as she neared, his one good eye softening with recognition. He didn't smile—not yet—but the relief was clear in his expression. "Emmalyn..."

She reached him, her breath catching in her throat. She touched his arm gently, her fingers tracing the edges of his tattered sleeve. "What happened? Where have you been? We've been..." Her voice faltered as she took in his appearance, the stark reality of what had happened to him settling in.

Noah's expression was unreadable, but there was a deep sadness in his eyes. He didn't immediately speak, instead lowering his head slightly as if to gather his thoughts.

"I was... I was close," he said quietly. "I got close to her. I found where they'd taken her. But I couldn't—couldn't get her out in time."

Emmalyn's heart tightened, her eyes filling with tears. "Noah, you don't have to—"

"No," he interrupted, his voice firm but pained. "I have to tell you. I need to tell you what happened. They took her to a place... a place that's even worse than we thought. There's a camp. A camp of the demon-worshippers. They're using people, Emmalyn. Not just for food, but for something worse."

Emmalyn felt a chill settle in her bones. "What do you mean? What are they doing to her?"

Noah's jaw tightened, and he looked away for a moment, as if trying to push away the images in his mind. "I don't know all the details. But I saw things... things I can't unsee. I fought to get her back, but they overwhelmed me. There were too many of them. I lost my eye and my hand in the fight. And they got away with her."

Emmalyn reached out and placed her hand on his shoulder, steadying herself. "You didn't fail her, Noah. You did everything you could. We're going to get her back."

Noah's expression softened, but there was a weariness in his eyes that spoke of his struggle to hold on to that very hope. "I almost didn't come back, Emmalyn. I thought about just leaving. But I couldn't. I had to make sure you knew what I found out. I couldn't just let her be lost."

"You didn't fail," Emmalyn repeated, her voice firm now. "You've found out more than we knew before. We can use that. And we'll get her back. We're not stopping."

He nodded slowly, his breath shaky. "I'll be ready to go again, once I'm healed. I'll help you get her back."

Emmalyn smiled, though it was tinged with sadness. "You don't need to do it alone. We're in this together."

The rest of the survivors had gathered around as the conversation unfolded, their expressions ranging from shock to sympathy as they took in the sight of Noah's injuries. Kelli stepped forward, her voice low but comforting. "We're glad you're back. You've been missed."

Wheels, who had been listening quietly, wheeled himself closer. "You've done more than anyone could ask, Noah. The road ahead won't be easy, but you've shown us all what true courage looks like. You're not alone in this fight."

Noah's lips tightened into a grim smile. "I couldn't leave her out there alone."

"We're all in this together," Wheels said, his voice steady. "And we will get her back. One step at a time."

Emmalyn stepped forward, her eyes still filled with concern. "You need rest, Noah. The fight will come, but you can't fight it on your own right now."

He nodded, though he didn't look happy about it. "I'll rest. But just long enough to heal and then we're going again. I won't stop until I bring her back."

Emmalyn placed her hand on his arm, her voice soft. "And you won't be alone. We'll all help. We'll bring Annabeth back. Together."

The group spent the rest of the evening setting up camp, Noah receiving the help he needed as they tended to his wounds. They knew the road ahead would be perilous, but now they had more than just hope—they had a plan. They had each other.

Emmalyn sat beside the fire later that night, her heart heavy with the weight of what Noah had shared. His absence had been a silent wound in their hearts, and now, seeing him back, knowing he was willing to fight again, was both a relief and a reminder of how much was still at stake.

She opened Annabeth's journal, her fingers tracing the familiar pages. *"The Lord is my shepherd; I shall not want."* The verse filled her with peace, even in the midst of the uncertainty they faced.

They had lost Annabeth, but they hadn't lost everything. They still had each other, and as long as they had that, they had a chance.

Noah had returned—wounded but not broken—and together, they would get Annabeth back.

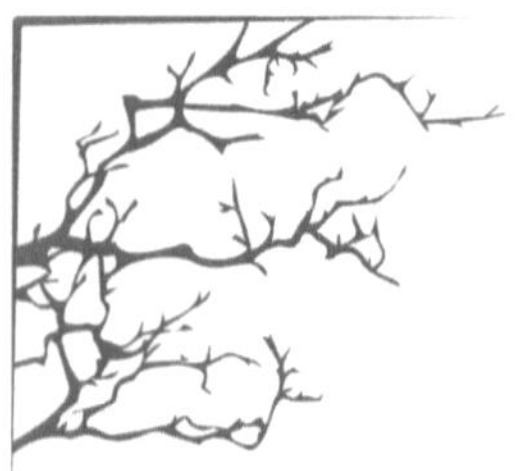

A New Bond

The morning sun broke through the trees, casting long rays of light across the camp. The group was quieter than usual, their thoughts lingering on Noah's return and the news he had brought. His injuries were a grim reminder of the dangers they faced, but his determination had reignited their resolve.

Noah sat on a low log near the fire, his one good eye scanning the camp. His missing hand and the patch over his left eye gave him the look of a warrior who had endured more than most, but his face was drawn with exhaustion. He barely moved, the weight of his injuries and his mission pressing heavily on him.

"Here," came a soft voice from behind him.

Noah turned to see Caitlyn, one of the younger survivors, holding a bowl of steaming broth. Her auburn hair was tied back in a loose braid, and her hazel eyes held a mix of concern and quiet determination. She was one of the newer members of the group, often working behind the scenes to help wherever she could, but she had rarely spoken directly to Noah until now.

"I made this for you," Caitlyn said, her voice calm but firm. "You need to eat."

Noah hesitated, his pride warring with his weariness. "I'm fine," he muttered, looking away.

"No, you're not," Caitlyn replied, her tone steady. She stepped closer, placing the bowl on the log beside him. "And that's okay. You've been through a lot. Let someone take care of you for a change."

He glanced up at her, surprised by the firmness in her voice. There was no pity in her gaze, only a quiet strength that he hadn't noticed before.

With a sigh, he picked up the bowl. "Thanks," he said gruffly.

Caitlyn smiled faintly, sitting down on a nearby rock. "You're welcome. You don't have to do everything on your own, you know."

Noah shrugged, taking a sip of the broth. "I've been on my own for a while. It's... hard to get used to this."

"This?" Caitlyn asked, tilting her head.

"People," Noah admitted. "Caring. Helping. I'm used to fighting, not... this."

"Well," Caitlyn said with a soft smile, "it's about time you let someone help you. You've done enough fighting for now."

Noah looked at her, his good eye narrowing slightly. "You don't even know me."

"I know enough," Caitlyn said simply. "I know you went out there alone to try to save Annabeth. I know you came back broken, but you didn't give up. That tells me a lot."

He was silent for a moment, her words settling over him like a blanket. "I didn't bring her back," he said finally, his voice low. "I failed."

Caitlyn leaned forward, her hazel eyes locking onto his. "You didn't fail. You did everything you could, and you made it back to us. That's not failure—that's courage."

Noah's lips tightened, but he didn't argue. He took another sip of the broth, the warmth spreading through him.

Over the next few days, Caitlyn became a constant presence at Noah's side. She helped him adjust to his injuries, finding ways to make simple tasks easier for him. She was patient but firm, never letting him sink too far into self-pity.

One afternoon, as she helped him rewrap the bandages on his arm, Noah glanced at her, his voice softer than usual. "Why are you doing this?"

"Because you need it," Caitlyn replied without hesitation.

"No," he said, shaking his head. "I mean... why you? There are plenty of others who could do this. Why bother with me?"

Caitlyn paused, her hands stilling for a moment. Then she looked up at him, her expression gentle. "Because I see something in you. Something worth fighting for. And because... I know what it's like to feel like you don't deserve help."

Noah frowned, studying her face. "What do you mean?"

Caitlyn sat back, letting out a quiet sigh. "Before all of this, I was... lost. I made mistakes—big ones. Hurt people I cared about. When everything fell apart, I thought it was my punishment, that I didn't deserve a second chance. But then... someone showed me mercy. Someone reminded me that God doesn't give up on us, even when we've given up on ourselves."

She met his gaze, her eyes steady. "You remind me of that. You've been through hell, but you're still here. You're still fighting. That means something."

Noah was quiet for a long moment, her words stirring something deep within him. Finally, he nodded, his voice barely above a whisper. "Thanks."

Caitlyn smiled, her expression soft. "Anytime."

As the days passed, the bond between them grew. Caitlyn's quiet strength balanced Noah's rough edges, and her unwavering support began to chip away at the walls he had built around himself. He found himself looking forward to their conversations, to the way she challenged him without judgment, to the warmth of her presence.

And Caitlyn, in turn, saw the man behind the scars—the warrior who carried the weight of the world on his shoulders but was still willing to fight for something greater than himself.

Their connection was unspoken but undeniable, a flicker of light in the midst of their shared darkness. And though neither of them said it out loud, they both knew that something was beginning to grow between them—something fragile but full of promise.

For now, they had a mission, a purpose that bound them together. But in the quiet moments between the battles, in the shared glances and quiet conversations, they found a different kind of strength: each other.

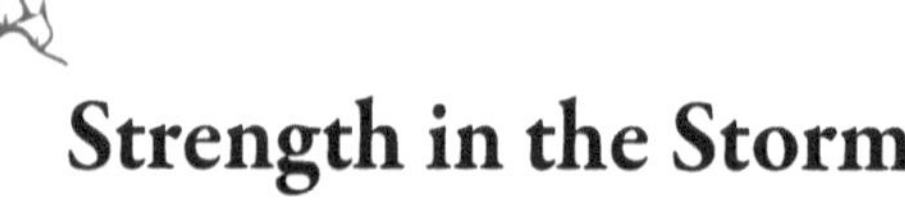

Strength in the Storm

The wind howled through the trees as the group moved carefully along the overgrown path, their steps muffled by the soft, damp earth. Dark clouds loomed overhead, threatening rain, and the air was thick with the tension of an approaching storm.

Emmalyn walked at the front of the group, her sword strapped to her back and Annabeth's journal tucked safely into her pack. She glanced over her shoulder, checking on the survivors trailing behind her. Wheels brought up the rear, his sharp eyes scanning the landscape for any signs of danger.

"Storm's coming," Kelli said quietly, falling into step beside Emmalyn.

"I know," Emmalyn replied, her gaze fixed on the horizon. "We need to find shelter soon."

Ahead of them, the path opened into a small clearing, where the remnants of an old stone chapel stood against the rising wind. Its walls were crumbling, and its roof had partially collapsed, but it still offered more protection than the open woods.

"That'll do," Wheels said, nodding toward the structure.

The group moved quickly, filing into the chapel as the first drops of rain began to fall. Inside, the air was cool and damp, but the stone walls muffled the sound of the storm outside, creating a small haven of quiet.

As the survivors settled in, Emmalyn noticed Noah sitting near one of the broken windows, staring out at the darkening sky. Caitlyn was beside him, speaking softly as she adjusted the sling he had fashioned for his injured arm. Their connection had become evident to the rest of the group over the past few days, though no one commented on it.

Emmalyn approached, her voice low. "How's he doing?"

Caitlyn looked up, offering a faint smile. "Stubborn as ever, but he's healing."

"I'm right here," Noah muttered, his tone dry but tinged with gratitude.

Emmalyn smirked. "Good. Then you can help me figure out what's next."

The group gathered near the center of the chapel, their faces illuminated by the soft glow of the golden lamp that rested on a makeshift altar. The light was a steady reminder of their mission, even in the midst of uncertainty.

"We're close," Emmalyn began, addressing the group. "Noah found where they took Annabeth. We know the direction we need to go, but we also know it won't be easy. They'll be waiting for us."

Kelli crossed her arms, her expression grim. "Do we have enough supplies for a fight? We're running low on food and water, and if we get cornered..."

"We'll manage," Wheels said firmly. "We've faced worse before, and we've made it through. This time won't be any different."

One of the younger survivors, a boy named Isaac, spoke up, his voice trembling. "What if... what if we don't find her? What if it's too late?"

Emmalyn's gaze softened as she knelt in front of him. "Isaac, I won't lie to you. This isn't going to be easy. But we have to trust that God brought us this far for a reason. We're not giving up on her. Not now, not ever."

The boy nodded, his fear giving way to determination.

As the group began to discuss their plans, Caitlyn moved quietly to one of the intact pews, sitting beside Noah. She leaned in close, her voice barely audible over the sound of the rain outside. "You don't have to do this alone, you know."

Noah glanced at her, his good eye narrowing slightly. "I'm not alone. I've got all of you."

"That's not what I meant," Caitlyn said softly. "I see the way you carry this—like it's all on your shoulders. But it's not. You've done more than anyone could have asked. It's okay to let us help you."

Noah hesitated, then nodded slowly. "I know. It's just... hard to let go."

Caitlyn reached out, her hand brushing against his. "You don't have to let go completely. Just enough to let someone else carry some of the weight."

A faint smile tugged at Noah's lips. "You're a stubborn one, you know that?"

"Takes one to know one," Caitlyn replied with a grin.

The sound of thunder rolled in the distance, a reminder of the storm raging outside. But within the chapel, there was a sense of calm—a quiet strength that bound them together.

Emmalyn returned to the front of the group, her voice steady as she addressed them once more. "Tonight, we rest. Tomorrow, we move. We're going to find Annabeth, and we're going to bring her home. Together."

The survivors nodded, their resolve solidifying despite the challenges ahead.

As the rain poured outside and the storm raged on, the group huddled close, drawing strength from one another and the light of the lamp. Their journey was far from over, but in that moment, they were reminded of what kept them going: faith, hope, and the unshakable belief that they were not alone.

Even in the storm, the light burned steady, a beacon of mercy and love guiding them forward. And they would follow it—no matter where it led.

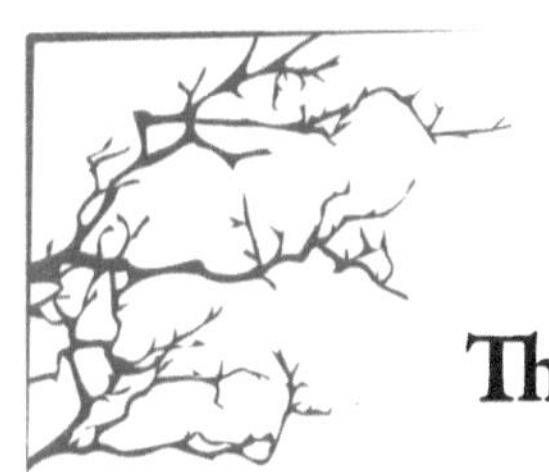

The Forge of Hope

The morning after the storm dawned gray and cold, the group stepped out of the ruined chapel to continue their journey. Though the rain had stopped, the ground was still soft and muddy, and the chill in the air seemed to seep into their bones.

Emmalyn led the way, her sharp eyes scanning the horizon for signs of danger or opportunity. Behind her, the survivors followed closely, their makeshift weapons clutched in hand, a reminder of how ill-prepared they were for the battles that awaited them.

The path took them through a dense forest and down into a narrow valley, where the remnants of an old settlement appeared, hidden among the trees. Smoke faintly curled from the chimney of one of the buildings, though it was unclear whether it was a recent fire or the lingering scent of long-abandoned work.

"That looks like a workshop," Kelli said, pointing to the largest building.

"Could be worth investigating," Emmalyn replied, tightening her grip on her sword hilt.

The group moved cautiously into the settlement, their steps quiet as they approached the building. The large wooden doors creaked open, revealing a sprawling workshop filled with tools, workbenches, and a massive forge. The faint warmth of embers in the hearth confirmed that someone had been here recently.

Colt stepped inside, his eyes lighting up as he took in the sight of the forge. "Well, I'll be," he muttered. "It's a blacksmith's shop. And it's still functional."

"It looks like no one's here now," Kelli said, peering around. "We should make the most of it while we can."

Wheels rolled into the building, his eyes narrowing as he studied the forge. "This could change everything," he said. "With the right tools, we can make real weapons. Things that will actually stand up against those demons."

Emmalyn nodded, her mind racing with possibilities. "Alright. Let's get to work. Search the place for supplies and bring everything to the forge. We don't know how long we have before we're discovered."

As the survivors fanned out to search the settlement, Colt and Wheels remained in the workshop, their hands itching to begin. Colt picked up a hammer, testing its weight with a smile.

"You've done this before," Wheels observed.

"Used to work in a smithy, years ago," Colt replied, setting the hammer down. "Never thought I'd be back at it, but here we are."

Wheels moved closer to the forge, running his hand along the edge of the anvil. "I worked in metal fabrication before everything went to hell. Mostly welding, but I know my way around steel." He glanced at Colt, a faint grin tugging at his lips. "Think we can make something worth wielding?"

Colt chuckled. "I think we can make something that'll give those demons a reason to think twice."

The two men got to work, sorting through the tools and scrap metal scattered around the workshop. Colt stoked the forge, feeding it with coal until the flames roared to life. Wheels inspected the piles of metal, selecting pieces that could be reforged into blades and shields.

The clang of hammer on metal echoed through the workshop as Colt began shaping a blade, the red-hot steel glowing brightly in the dim light. Sparks flew with each strike, the rhythmic sound drawing the attention of the others.

Emmalyn entered, watching as Colt carefully folded and shaped the metal. "What are you making?" she asked.

"A real sword," Colt replied, not looking up. "One that won't snap the second you clash with a demon."

Emmalyn raised an eyebrow. "You're saying my sword isn't good enough?"

"I'm saying you deserve better," Colt said with a smirk. "And you're about to get it."

Nearby, Wheels was working on a shield, welding pieces of scrap metal together with practiced precision. Clara stood by his side, handing him tools and watching in awe.

"You've got a real gift," Clara said softly.

"Just doing what needs to be done," Wheels replied. "If we're going to survive what's ahead, we need better than sticks and scavenged knives."

As the hours passed, the survivors gathered in the workshop, watching as Colt and Wheels transformed raw materials into weapons and armor. The once-silent forge now roared with life, a symbol of resilience and determination.

By evening, the group stood armed with weapons far superior to the ones they had carried before. Emmalyn held her new sword, testing its weight with a look of satisfaction.

"This is incredible," she said, turning to Colt. "You've outdone yourself."

Colt shrugged, though there was a glimmer of pride in his expression. "It's just metal and fire. The real fight is up to you."

Wheels handed a finished shield to Kelli, who inspected it with an approving nod. "This will do nicely," she said.

Emmalyn stepped forward, addressing the group. "These weapons are more than tools. They're a reminder of what we're fighting for. To protect each other. To stand against the darkness. To bring Annabeth home."

The survivors nodded, their resolve renewed. They had been battered and broken, but now they stood stronger, their unity forged alongside their weapons.

As the night fell and the fire of the forge began to dim, Emmalyn felt a spark of hope ignite within her. They were ready—not just to survive, but to fight for something greater. Together, they would face whatever lay ahead.

And they would not stop until Annabeth was home.

Preparing for the Fight

The morning air was crisp and carried the faint smell of coal and metal from the forge they had worked tirelessly in the day before. The survivors were gathered in the clearing outside the workshop, their newly forged weapons glinting in the early sunlight. Though they looked the part of a battle-ready group, Emmalyn knew they were far from prepared.

Colt and Wheels stood at the front of the group, their faces set with determination. Both men had seen combat in their own ways, and now they were united in a shared purpose: to prepare the survivors for the fight of their lives.

"Alright," Colt began, his voice firm. "It's one thing to hold a weapon. It's another thing entirely to know how to use it." He gestured to the group. "Most of you haven't been in a real fight before. If we're going to face demons—or anything else—we need to know how to fight together."

Wheels rolled forward, his sharp brown eyes scanning the group. "This isn't about strength or size. It's about strategy. About working as a unit. If you can't trust the person beside you, you're as good as dead. So, let's make sure we're ready before we charge into anything."

Colt began by demonstrating basic sword techniques, his movements precise and efficient. He showed the group how to block, parry, and strike, breaking down each motion so even the youngest survivors could follow.

"Don't swing wildly," he instructed, adjusting Isaac's grip on his blade. "Controlled movements. Precision over power. A wild swing leaves you open, and the demons won't hesitate to take advantage of that."

Isaac nodded, his brow furrowed in concentration as he practiced the movements Colt had shown him.

Meanwhile, Wheels worked with those carrying shields, showing them how to form a defensive line. He rolled along the row, tapping shields with his staff to test their stability.

"Hold steady," Wheels said, his voice calm but commanding. "A shield wall is only as strong as its weakest link. If one of you falters, the whole line breaks."

Kelli, who had taken to her shield with surprising skill, stood at the center of the line, her posture firm. "We've got this," she said, glancing at the others. "Just stay together."

Clara practiced with a spear, her movements awkward at first but gradually improving under Wheels' guidance. "Don't overreach," he told her. "A spear keeps your enemy at a distance. Use that to your advantage."

As the morning wore on, Colt and Wheels shifted the focus from individual techniques to team tactics. They set up mock scenarios, pitting half the group against the other to simulate real combat situations.

"Communication is key," Colt said as the survivors took their positions. "If you see something, call it out. If someone needs help, you cover them. No one fights alone."

The first few drills were chaotic, with shouts and missed opportunities leading to disarray. But with each round, the group improved. They began to move as a unit, covering each other's weaknesses and reinforcing their strengths.

"Better," Wheels said after the fourth drill, nodding in approval. "You're starting to get it."

By midday, the group was sweaty and tired, but their confidence had grown. Emmalyn watched from the sidelines, her heart swelling with pride at their progress. These people, who had once been scattered and afraid, were becoming something more—a force to be reckoned with.

During a break, Emmalyn approached Colt and Wheels, who were discussing the next phase of training.

"You're doing great with them," she said, handing Colt a canteen of water.

Colt took a sip, wiping his brow. "They're learning fast. Faster than I expected."

"Not just because of us," Wheels added, glancing at Emmalyn. "You've been leading them since the start. They trust you. That's why they're willing to fight."

Emmalyn shook her head. "They trust all of us. And they're fighting because they know what's at stake. Annabeth... the mission... it's bigger than any one of us."

Colt nodded, his expression softening. "True. But you're the one keeping them together. Don't forget that."

Emmalyn smiled faintly, though the weight of their words settled heavily on her.

As the sun dipped lower in the sky, Colt and Wheels called the group together for one final exercise.

"This time, we're simulating an ambush," Colt said, pointing to a series of markers they had set up in the clearing. "You'll be outnumbered and outflanked. Your job is to hold the line and protect the group at all costs."

The survivors exchanged nervous glances, but they nodded in unison, ready to face the challenge.

The drill began with Colt and Wheels leading the "enemy" force, using their knowledge of tactics to press the group from all sides. Emmalyn took charge of the defensive line, calling out orders and coordinating movements.

"Left flank, hold steady!" she shouted as Clara and Kelli reinforced their position. "Isaac, watch your right!"

Despite the pressure, the survivors held their ground, their teamwork and training paying off. When the exercise ended, Colt and Wheels called them together, their expressions filled with approval.

"You did good," Colt said, his voice steady. "Real good. You're ready for what's coming."

Wheels nodded. "Remember what you've learned today. Trust each other. Fight smart. And never, ever give up."

As the group settled down for the evening, their spirits were higher than they had been in weeks. They were still outnumbered and outmatched by the forces they faced, but they were no longer defenseless.

Sitting by the fire, Emmalyn looked around at the survivors—her family now. They had come so far, and though the road ahead was uncertain, she knew they would face it together.

Colt and Wheels sat nearby, quietly discussing the day's progress and the next steps in their journey.

"You think they're ready?" Wheels asked.

"They're as ready as they'll ever be," Colt replied. "And they've got something the demons don't—each other."

Emmalyn closed her eyes briefly, sending up a silent prayer. For Annabeth. For the group. For the strength to keep going.

Because now, they weren't just survivors. They were warriors.

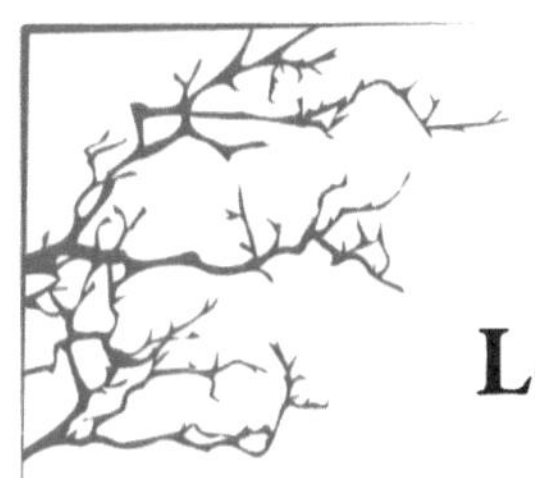

Love in the Chaos

The massive demon bore down on the group, its fiery eyes blazing with malice. Its roars shook the ground, sending tremors through the camp as it moved with terrifying speed. Emmalyn, Noah, and Colt stood their ground, their weapons ready, but the sheer size and power of the creature dwarfed their resolve.

"Keep it distracted!" Emmalyn shouted, lunging forward with her sword. She struck at the demon's legs, her blade cutting deep, but it barely flinched.

Noah darted to the side, his movements quick despite his injuries. He swung his blade, slicing across the creature's flank, but it retaliated with a powerful swipe of its claw, sending him sprawling to the ground.

"Noah!" Emmalyn cried, her heart leaping as she saw him struggle to rise.

The demon turned its attention to Noah, its massive form towering over him as it raised a claw to strike. Noah gritted his teeth, raising his sword in a last, desperate attempt to defend himself.

But before the demon could strike, a fierce cry rang out, cutting through the chaos.

"Get away from him!"

Caitlyn appeared from the shadows, her spear gleaming as she charged the demon with unrelenting force. She drove the weapon into its side, the impact sending a shockwave through the creature's body.

The demon let out a deafening roar, its fiery gaze shifting to Caitlyn. She didn't falter, pulling her spear free and driving it into the beast again, this time aiming for its throat. The creature stumbled, its movements growing sluggish as the light in its eyes began to fade.

Noah stared in disbelief as Caitlyn delivered the final blow, her spear piercing the demon's heart. The massive creature let out a final, guttural roar before collapsing to the ground, its body dissolving into ash.

Caitlyn turned, her chest heaving as she met Noah's gaze. For a moment, the world seemed to stop, the chaos of the battle fading into the background.

"Noah," she said breathlessly, dropping her spear and rushing to his side.

"I'm fine," Noah muttered, though his voice was shaky. "I think."

"You're an idiot," Caitlyn said, her voice trembling with a mix of relief and anger. "Charging into a demon like that. What were you thinking?"

"I was thinking we didn't have a choice," Noah replied, his good eye locking onto hers. "What are you doing here? I thought you were holding the line."

Caitlyn knelt beside him, her hands hovering over his injuries. "I couldn't stay back. Not when I knew you might not make it. I had to come."

Noah opened his mouth to reply, but before he could say anything, Caitlyn leaned in and kissed him. The world seemed to blur around them, the sounds of the battle fading into the distance.

For a moment, there was nothing but the two of them—their shared fear, their relief, and the unspoken connection that had grown between them.

When Caitlyn pulled back, her cheeks flushed, she searched his face for a reaction.

Noah blinked, stunned, but a faint smile tugged at the corners of his lips. "You've got terrible timing, you know that?"

"Yeah," Caitlyn said, a small laugh escaping her. "But it worked."

Emmalyn's voice broke through the moment. "As touching as this is, we're not done yet!"

Caitlyn helped Noah to his feet, his arm slung over her shoulder for support. He winced but managed to stay upright, his determination unwavering.

"We'll finish this," Noah said, his voice steady despite the pain.

Together, they turned back to the fray, ready to rejoin the fight. The demon might have fallen, but the battle was far from over. And now, they fought with renewed strength—not just for survival, but for each other.

Victory and Redemption

The final remnants of the demon horde fell with guttural shrieks, their bodies dissolving into ash as the survivors pressed their attack. With the massive demon slain and its sinister presence vanquished, the tide of the battle turned in the group's favor.

Emmalyn drove her sword into one last demon, stepping back as its form crumbled before her. She turned, her breath heavy, and surveyed the battlefield. The survivors stood together, battered but alive, their weapons raised in triumph.

"It's over," Colt said, his voice steady as he wiped sweat from his brow. "We did it."

Cheers rose from the group, the sound a mix of relief and exhilaration.

Wheels rolled toward Emmalyn, his shield still braced against his arm. "They fought well," he said, nodding toward the group of rescued survivors huddled near the outskirts of the camp.

"They fought for their lives," Emmalyn replied, her voice heavy with emotion. "And now, we have to show them why."

Annabeth, leaning on Clara for support, stepped forward, her face pale but determined. "They don't know," she said softly. "They've been living in fear for so long, they don't understand what it means to have hope. We have to show them."

Emmalyn nodded. "We will."

As the group gathered around the campfire that evening, the atmosphere was solemn yet charged with a sense of purpose. The survivors sat together, their faces illuminated by the flickering flames.

Many were silent, still processing the horrors they had endured and the battle they had survived.

Emmalyn stood at the center of the group, Annabeth by her side. She held Annabeth's journal in her hands, the worn leather a reminder of the faith that had guided them this far.

"When we came here," Emmalyn began, her voice steady, "we didn't know if we'd make it out alive. The odds were against us—hundreds to one. But we didn't fight this battle alone."

She opened the journal, flipping to a familiar passage. "In Judges 7, Gideon faced a battle just like ours. His army was outnumbered, but God told him to send most of his soldiers home. He was left with only three hundred men. Three hundred against an entire army. And they won, not because of their strength, but because of their faith."

She paused, letting the words sink in. "Tonight, we stand here because of that same faith. We believed that God brought us here for a reason. And He did. He brought us here to save not just ourselves, but each other."

The survivors murmured softly, their eyes reflecting a mix of gratitude and wonder.

Annabeth stepped forward, her voice quiet but filled with conviction. "I know many of you have questions—about why this happened, about what comes next. I can't promise to have all the answers. But I do know this: God hasn't abandoned us. He's been with us every step of the way, even when it felt like we were alone."

She held out her hands, palms up. "If you're ready to learn more, if you want to understand what it means to have faith, we're here for you. This isn't the end of the journey—it's just the beginning."

Over the next several days, the group worked to rebuild trust and foster hope among the survivors. They shared stories of their own struggles and triumphs, using Annabeth's journal and passages from the Bible to guide their conversations.

Caitlyn and Noah took on the role of teaching small groups, using their bond to show the strength that came from faith and unity.

"This isn't about being perfect," Caitlyn said during one session. "It's about understanding that we're loved, no matter what. God doesn't wait for us to fix ourselves before He helps us—He meets us where we are."

Noah, his arm still bandaged, nodded. "I used to think I had to do everything on my own. That asking for help was a weakness. But I've learned that strength doesn't come from pretending you're okay. It comes from trusting that God will get you through."

Emmalyn and Wheels focused on the larger group, teaching them how to defend themselves while also reinforcing the importance of compassion and mercy.

"We're not just fighting for survival," Wheels said during a training session. "We're fighting to protect the light inside each of us. That light is what makes us human. It's what connects us to God."

By the time the group was ready to leave the camp, the survivors had transformed. They were no longer a scattered, frightened crowd—they were a community bound by shared faith and a newfound sense of purpose.

As they set out on the road together, Annabeth walked beside Emmalyn, her steps steadier now. "Do you think they'll hold on to what they've learned?" Annabeth asked, glancing back at the group.

"They will," Emmalyn replied, her voice filled with quiet confidence. "Because it's not just about what we've taught them. It's about what they've seen—what they've lived. They've faced the darkness, and they've come out stronger."

Annabeth smiled faintly. "It feels like a miracle."

"It is," Emmalyn said, her gaze fixed on the horizon. "And it's just the beginning."

With the group behind them and the future stretching out before them, the survivors marched forward, their faith as their guide and their hope as their strength. Together, they would face whatever lay ahead, knowing that they were never truly alone.

The Road to Resurgam

M onths passed since the battle for Annabeth, and though the weight of their journey had not lightened, the survivors had begun to find new purpose. The horrors of the past still haunted them, but they carried with them something stronger than fear—hope. It burned quietly in their hearts, steady and unyielding, even as they pressed forward through uncertain landscapes.

The group moved slowly, deliberately, always on the lookout for a place to settle—a safe haven where they could rebuild. They were no longer just survivors; they were a community. They had learned to trust each other, to rely on their faith, and to protect those around them. They had come to understand that what they were fighting for was not just survival, but the future—the chance to create something new from the ashes of their old lives.

"Where are we going, Emmalyn?" Kelli asked one afternoon, glancing around at the endless stretches of grass and forest. "We've been traveling for months. It feels like we're just drifting."

"We're not drifting," Emmalyn replied, her voice steady. "We're searching. Searching for a place where we can rebuild. A place where we can begin again."

"And what's it called?" Noah asked, his arm still in a makeshift sling, but his steps strong and determined.

"Resurgam," Emmalyn said quietly, her eyes scanning the horizon. "It means 'I shall rise again.' A new beginning."

"That's a good name," Noah said with a half-smile, glancing back at the group. "A place where we can start over. A place that's not just about surviving, but living."

"Exactly," Emmalyn said. She had been carrying the vision of Resurgam in her heart for months—ever since the battle that freed them all. It wasn't just a place; it was a symbol of everything they had fought for: redemption, rebirth, and hope. But finding it, she knew, wouldn't be easy.

The survivors trekked through forests, crossed rivers, and passed through abandoned villages, always searching. They didn't have a map, no clear direction—only the belief that somewhere, hidden in the vast, desolate lands, there was a place that could become their new home.

Along the way, they met other survivors, some more hopeful than others, but each with their own story. Some joined the group, others chose to stay behind, hesitant to leave the familiarity of the ruins they called home. But for those who continued with them, the idea of Resurgam was a beacon—a promise of something better.

One evening, as the group gathered around a campfire, Annabeth spoke up. "We've been through so much. Sometimes I don't know how we're still going." Her voice was quiet, thoughtful. "But every time I think about giving up, I remember what we're fighting for. Not just to survive. But to build something. To rebuild everything that was lost."

"We're not just surviving anymore," Kelli said, her face reflecting the conviction in Annabeth's words. "We're living. And we're building. One step at a time."

Emmalyn glanced at the others, her heart swelling with pride. They had come so far. Every battle, every hardship, every loss had brought them here—not just as individuals, but as a family. And now, Resurgam wasn't just a dream; it was their future.

After months of travel, their hopes began to feel like a distant star—flickering, almost unreachable. But one evening, just as the sun began to set, casting a warm golden light over the land, they crested a ridge and saw it.

Before them lay a valley, lush and green, with a wide river winding its way through the landscape. The valley was sheltered by towering mountains on either side, the peaks shrouded in mist. It was a place of peace, untouched by the horrors they had encountered along the way.

"This is it," Emmalyn said, her voice filled with awe. "This is Resurgam."

The group stood in silence, taking in the sight. The land was fertile, with rolling hills and rich soil. A forest bordered one side of the valley, offering shelter and protection. To the east, the river could be used for water and fishing. It was a place full of promise, a sanctuary where they could begin again.

"We've found it," Colt said, his voice rough with emotion. "After everything... we've found it."

"We've found home," Noah said, looking over at Emmalyn with a quiet smile.

"We have," she agreed, her eyes misty. "Now, we rebuild."

The next few days were filled with work—marking the boundaries of their new home, gathering resources, and beginning the slow process of creating shelter. Emmalyn and the others worked side by side, their determination as strong as ever. They had no grand blueprints, no plans set in stone. They simply worked with what they had, relying on each other's skills and strength.

Colt and Wheels took the lead in designing the first structures, using the materials they found in the valley to build sturdy homes and fortifications. Noah helped with the heavy lifting, despite his injuries, while Kelli and Caitlyn worked on gathering food and water.

Annabeth, her strength returning slowly but steadily, organized the group, ensuring that everyone had a task, that nothing went to waste.

"There's so much to do," Kelli said one evening, sitting beside Emmalyn. "I don't know where to start."

Emmalyn smiled, watching the group work. "We start by doing what we can. Every step we take here is another piece of the foundation. We build a home. And we build it together."

As the sun set behind the mountains, casting a warm glow over the valley, Emmalyn allowed herself a moment to breathe. They were no longer wandering. They were no longer running. They had found their place, their home, and they were building something that would last—a place where they could live, not just survive.

The vision of Resurgam—of rebirth, of a fresh start—was no longer just a distant dream. It was reality. And as the group gathered around the fire that night, Emmalyn looked around at the faces of those she had fought beside, those she had come to love like family.

This was only the beginning. They had risen from the ashes, and together, they would build a future brighter than anything they had ever known.

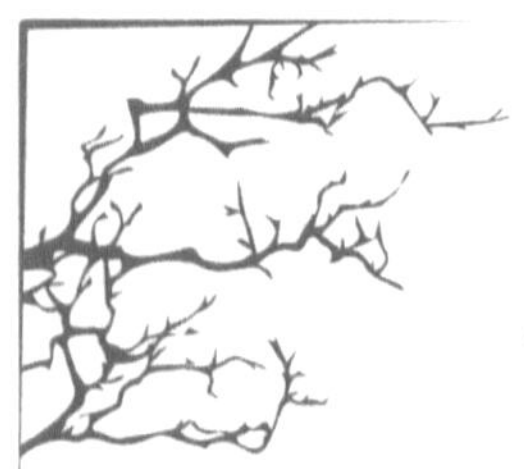

The First Stone

Days turned into weeks, and the survivors worked tirelessly to transform the fertile valley into a sanctuary. What was once a barren stretch of land, marked by scars of the past, now began to bloom under their collective efforts. The foundation of Resurgam was being laid—one stone, one timber, one dream at a time.

Amidst all their labor, Emmalyn knew there was something vital they had to establish first—something that would bind their community together. It wasn't just a physical structure they needed to build; it was a space for faith, a place to nurture the hope that had kept them going. It was time for the church.

The idea came naturally—Resurgam needed more than just shelter. It needed a cornerstone, a symbol that they were building a future, not just surviving. It was faith that had guided them through the darkest days, and it would be faith that helped them thrive here, together.

"Let's build a church," Emmalyn said one evening, gathering the group around the small campfire where they had been resting after a long day's work.

"A church?" Colt asked, wiping his brow and looking up from where he had been working on a foundation. "In the middle of nowhere? Isn't that a bit... much?"

"No," Emmalyn replied with certainty. "This place is a symbol of rebirth—Resurgam. We're not just rebuilding houses, we're rebuilding ourselves, our community. A church will remind us of what we're fighting for."

Wheels, who had been rolling nearby, stopped and nodded. "A place for everyone to come together and reflect on what we've survived... I like it."

Noah, still working on rehabilitation from his injuries, looked up from where he had been tying off some supplies. His voice was steady, full of resolve. "I think it's the right thing to do. We've survived this long because we held on to something more than just our lives—we held on to our faith."

Emmalyn's eyes met Noah's, and there was a quiet understanding between them. "We've all made it this far together. And together, we'll keep going. With a church, we're not just building homes. We're creating a foundation for this new life."

And so, the plan for the church began.

The survivors worked side by side, carving out the foundation of the church. They used wood from the surrounding forest and stones from the riverbed, constructing a simple but sturdy building. The work was hard, but there was an underlying sense of purpose that carried them through.

Emmalyn, Annabeth, and Kelli took the lead on the design. The church would be modest, nothing fancy, but it would be a place where people could come together for worship, reflection, and community. It would be a structure that stood firm, like their faith.

As the church took shape, something began to shift within the group. The survivors, once a fractured collection of strangers, began to find a deeper connection—not just to the land, but to each other. The act of building something together, creating a new beginning from the ashes of the past, was a powerful thing. And in that space, a quiet sense of belonging began to grow.

While the walls of the church were going up, the survivors were starting to heal. Not just physically, but emotionally. The bonds that had been formed during their hardest days were now turning into something stronger—unity, hope, and shared faith.

One evening, as the last walls of the church were nearing completion, Emmalyn paused and looked around at the group. The sun was setting, casting a warm golden light over the work they had done, and she realized that this wasn't just a building. It was a monument to their resilience.

"We're not just surviving anymore," she said, her voice filled with quiet pride. "We're living. And we're building something lasting here. Something that will remind us of what we've fought for."

As the group gathered to celebrate their progress, Noah walked up to Caitlyn, his gaze steady and sure. Caitlyn, who had been by his side throughout this journey, met his eyes, her heart full of the unspoken connection that had grown between them over the past few months. They had fought side by side, and in those quiet moments, they had become more than just survivors—they had become partners in this new life they were building.

"Noah?" Caitlyn asked softly, her brow furrowed in confusion.

He smiled, though it was tinged with nervousness. "I... I've been thinking about this for a long time," he said, his voice rough. "We've both been through so much, and I can't imagine doing this without you by my side."

Caitlyn's heart skipped a beat. She knew exactly where this was going. She had felt it too, the pull between them, the bond that had formed not out of need, but out of something deeper—love, trust, and shared strength.

Noah took a deep breath and dropped to one knee, his hand reaching for hers. "Caitlyn, will you marry me? Will you stay by my side as we build this future—together?"

Caitlyn's breath caught in her throat. She looked around at the group, at the church they had just begun to build, and then back at Noah. Everything they had fought for, everything they had survived, had led them to this moment.

"Yes," she whispered, her voice trembling. "Yes, I'll marry you."

Noah smiled, a deep, genuine smile that reached his eyes, and he pulled her into an embrace. The group around them cheered, their voices ringing out in support. It wasn't just a celebration of their union, but of everything they had accomplished together. Their love wasn't just for survival—it was for a future, a future they would build with faith and strength.

The church was finished. It stood proudly at the heart of the valley, a symbol of everything they had endured and everything they had yet to accomplish. The survivors gathered there for the first time, their faces filled with hope and anticipation.

Emmalyn stood at the front, her heart full as she watched the group take their seats. She had led them through so much, but now, it was time for them to lead themselves—to take what they had learned, what they had fought for, and carry it forward into the future.

Noah and Caitlyn sat side by side, their hands intertwined. Noah had asked her to marry him, and she had said yes—her heart full of love, her mind full of hope. They were not just survivors; they were a family, and this church, this place they had built together, was theirs.

Emmalyn took a deep breath, her voice steady as she began to speak. "We've come so far. We've fought for our lives. We've built a home. And now, together, we will build a future. This is Resurgam. A place where we rise again, stronger than before."

The survivors stood together, their voices rising in unison. And as they stood in the church they had built, their faith and hope stronger than ever, Emmalyn knew this was just the beginning. Together, they would rise, together they would rebuild, and together they would make a home out of the ashes.

A Union of Hope and Faith

The sun shone brightly over Resurgam as the survivors gathered in the newly built church, their hearts full of hope and gratitude. The land, once barren and ravaged, had been transformed through their collective effort. They had built a home, a community, and now, with the church rising at its center, they had created a place for faith to grow—a symbol of renewal.

Today was a day for celebration. It was not just a union of two people, but a symbol of the future they were building together, a promise that despite everything they had endured, love, hope, and faith would lead them forward.

Noah and Caitlyn stood at the altar, hands clasped, facing each other. Around them, the survivors stood in quiet anticipation, their eyes filled with pride. The church, still fresh and new, had been adorned with simple wildflowers picked from the fields, a reminder of the beauty they were rebuilding from the ashes. The walls, although plain, had a unique touch—scrawled on the wooden beams and frames were Bible verses, prayers, and messages of hope that the survivors had written during the construction. Each verse was a promise, each prayer a plea for protection and blessing.

"We've built this place together," Emmalyn said, standing at the front with Annabeth beside her, "and we've filled it with our faith. It is not just walls and timber, but a place where we can gather as one family, and remember what we've fought for—what we continue to fight for."

The survivors had all contributed in their own way. As the church's frame went up, each person had written their favorite verse or a prayer on a beam, a wall, or the rafters. These simple, heartfelt words were now embedded in the structure, a part of the church that would never fade, even as the world outside continued to change.

Colt stepped forward, standing beside the couple with a warm smile. He had seen many things in his time, but today, he saw something he hadn't in years—hope, not just for survival, but for something more.

"This church isn't just wood and nails," Colt said, his voice resonating in the stillness. "It's our story, written in prayer, in faith, and in the love we've shared to get here. It's a symbol of our journey together, of the promises we've made to one another and to God."

Wheels, positioned at the pulpit, nodded in agreement. "We've come through darkness, but here, we build the light. And that light is what will guide us in the days to come. Today is a reminder that no matter how hard the journey, no matter how many battles we face, we stand together, bound by the faith that has carried us this far."

The vows began, and Noah turned to Caitlyn, his heart pounding in his chest. "I've seen things I never thought I would, and I've been through things that I never thought I could survive," he said, his voice rough but filled with sincerity. "But the one thing I've learned is that we don't walk this road alone. You've stood by me, Caitlyn. You've fought with me, and you've loved me. With you, I know I'm not just surviving. I'm living. And I promise to spend the rest of my life with you, loving you, and building this future together."

Caitlyn smiled softly, tears glistening in her eyes. "I thought I lost everything," she whispered. "But then I found you. And now, I know, we're stronger together. I promise to always stand by you, no matter what comes next, because with you, I am whole. And I will love you all the days of my life."

Their hands intertwined, and as they exchanged rings, the survivors around them stood in silence, the significance of the moment settling in. This wasn't just a wedding—it was a covenant, a commitment to one another and to the future they were creating together.

Emmalyn couldn't help but smile as she looked at the couple, her heart swelling with pride and hope. They were not just getting married—they were laying down the foundation for the future of Resurgam, a future built on love, faith, and unity.

As the ceremony ended, the newlyweds turned to the crowd, their faces glowing with joy. The survivors applauded, their voices full of encouragement, and Emmalyn turned to see the joy in the faces of everyone around her. The people who had been through so much now stood united, not just by circumstance, but by a shared belief in what they were building here.

After the wedding, the survivors gathered to offer their prayers and blessings for the church. Each person who had contributed to the church's construction—each verse, each prayer written on the walls—came forward, touching the beams and praying silently for what they hoped for this place to become.

Emmalyn watched as the survivors wrote one final prayer on the last beam. She picked up a marker and wrote a simple verse, one she'd found solace in many times throughout their journey:

"For I know the plans I have for you, declares the Lord, plans to prosper you and not to harm you, plans to give you a hope and a future." – Jeremiah 29:11

With that, she stepped back, taking a deep breath. She knew this church would be more than just a place of worship—it would be a place of refuge, of comfort, and of strength for generations to come.

Later that evening, as the sun began to set over the valley, Wheels stood at the pulpit, his expression serious but filled with wisdom. The joy of the wedding and the hope of the church's completion still hung in the air, but now was the time to prepare for what lay ahead.

"This is a new beginning," Wheels said, his voice steady. "But we cannot forget the world we've come from, or the trials that still await us. This is the beginning of our lives here in Resurgam, but there are darker days ahead. The Great Tribulation is still before us. And while we stand in peace today, we must always be vigilant."

The group grew quiet, the weight of Wheels' words settling over them. The world beyond Resurgam was still chaotic, still broken, and the peace they had found here could be threatened at any moment.

Wheels paused, his gaze sweeping over the group. "We've been given this chance—this beautiful place to rebuild—but we must remember that our true fight is not against flesh and blood. The true battle is spiritual. And when the time comes, when the world descends into chaos, when the final trials arrive, we must stand firm in our faith."

He raised his hands, his voice ringing with authority. "But take heart, because we will not face these trials alone. Christ will return, and His army will be called. And we, the children of God, will stand with Him. Our battle will be His. And with Him, we will overcome."

The room was silent, the weight of the prophecy settling over the survivors. But there was no fear in their hearts—not anymore. They had come this far because of their faith, and it was their faith that would carry them through the battles to come.

Noah and Caitlyn stood together, their hands clasped, ready to face whatever the future held. Resurgam had risen again. And together, with faith as their guide, they would stand strong until the very end.

Fortifying Resurgam

The days following the wedding had been filled with both work and reflection. The survivors now understood that Resurgam wasn't just a place of rest—it was a stronghold. A sanctuary that had to be fortified, not just with walls and weapons, but with faith and resolve.

The church, completed and filled with the prayers of those who had built it, stood as the heart of Resurgam. It was a symbol of hope, but it was also the foundation of something far more important. The battle for their future was far from over, and as much as they had fought to build this new life, they knew they would need to fight to protect it.

"We've built a home," Emmalyn said, standing at the front of the gathered group one morning, her voice steady as she addressed the survivors. "But we have to remember that the enemy isn't gone. The demons, the forces that once threatened us, will come again. And when they do, we need to be ready."

The survivors had gathered in the town square, a place that, while still in progress, was already beginning to feel like the heart of the community. They stood before the growing church, listening intently as Emmalyn spoke.

"We are in a place of peace now, yes," she continued, "but peace doesn't mean we stop preparing. It means we strengthen our resolve, and we fortify this place. Resurgam will be a beacon, a place where we protect not just ourselves but all who seek refuge."

Emmalyn's words resonated deeply with everyone. The light they had built here was fragile, and though the valley felt safe, they knew that their safety depended on how well they prepared for the battles that would come.

Colt, Wheels, and Noah took the lead in fortifying the town, using their collective knowledge of construction, defense, and strategy. With their newfound strength, they began to design the outer walls—strong, high enough to keep enemies at bay, but also allowing for escape routes and entry points should they need to fall back. The survivors worked together, cutting timber, hauling stone, and assembling what would eventually become a fortress.

"We'll need to build a perimeter," Colt said as he surveyed the land, a map of the valley spread before him. "A wall around the town, but also guard towers at key points. If we can get high ground, we can see anything approaching for miles."

"No stone left unturned," Wheels added, his eyes narrowing as he looked out over the valley. "We need traps, hidden positions, and lookouts. If they attack, we won't be caught off guard."

Noah, despite his injuries, joined them in planning the defense. "We've fought together before. We'll fight together again. I know how to hold a line, but we need to be strategic. If we're going to stand a chance against what's coming, we'll need every hand."

"We'll need all the supplies we can get," Kelli chimed in as she stepped forward. "Food, water, ammunition. It's not just the walls we need to focus on—it's making sure we can survive once the battle starts."

The survivors, having already begun to form a close-knit, well-coordinated community, rallied to the cause. The strong worked together to build, the skilled crafted weapons, and others began gathering supplies, knowing that the strength of their community would come from the unity of their efforts.

Meanwhile, Emmalyn and the others began training the group in battle tactics. They knew that when the enemy came, they would have to defend not just their walls, but their loved ones and their faith.

"We fight as a unit," Emmalyn said during one of their training sessions, her voice ringing through the open air. "When the enemy strikes, we need to move together. One breaks, and the whole line breaks. We need to know each other's strengths and weaknesses. That's the only way we survive."

Colt led the combat training, teaching the group basic combat techniques with swords, shields, and spears. They practiced blocking, parrying, and striking with precision.

"Speed, accuracy, and strength in unity," he said, demonstrating a defensive stance. "Each strike must be purposeful. You're not just swinging wildly—you're creating an opening. And you protect the person next to you, just as they protect you."

Noah worked with the younger survivors, teaching them the importance of focus in battle. "The enemy is relentless. You can't fight back with fear. You need to know your weapon, know your movement, and fight with purpose."

Wheels helped with logistics, organizing the storage of food, water, and medical supplies. "When the battle comes, you can't afford to run out of anything," he said, making sure that the survivors understood the importance of stockpiling. "A well-stocked town is a defended town."

One evening, after a particularly intense training session, Wheels called the group together. They had made significant progress on the walls and had completed their first round of training, but he knew there was something else they needed to focus on—their hearts.

"Faith isn't just something we say," Wheels began, standing at the front of the group, the evening sun casting long shadows across the land. "It's something we live. The battle that's coming will test us in ways we don't yet understand. The temptation to fear, to doubt, will be great. But we have something stronger than any enemy. We have our faith."

He paused, looking out over the survivors. They had grown stronger, more resolute, but there was still an air of uncertainty in some of their eyes. It was natural. They had fought to survive, but they hadn't yet seen what was truly coming.

"We must remain united in our faith, in our trust in God's plan. We must continue to prepare—not just our bodies, but our spirits. The trials ahead will be difficult, but with faith in Christ, we will stand firm. We will rise."

The survivors stood in silence, absorbing his words. For some, it was a reminder of everything they had been through. For others, it was a call to arms—a call to rise up in faith, to stand together, and to face whatever darkness lay ahead.

As weeks passed, the walls of Resurgam grew taller and stronger. Watchtowers were erected, gates were reinforced, and a network of traps and escape routes were set into place. The survivors continued to train, growing stronger, faster, and more skilled in the art of defense. They knew that no matter how strong the walls were, their true strength would come from the bond they had forged with one another and the faith they held in their hearts.

Resurgam was no longer just a dream. It was becoming a fortress—a place that would stand against the darkness, not because of its walls, but because of the people who had built it, and the God who watched over them.

And as they worked, Emmalyn couldn't shake the feeling that the days ahead would demand everything from them. But she also knew that with each brick, each prayer, each act of preparation, they were readying themselves—not just for survival, but for the final victory.

Their fight was far from over. But in Resurgam, they would stand together, and in faith, they would rise.

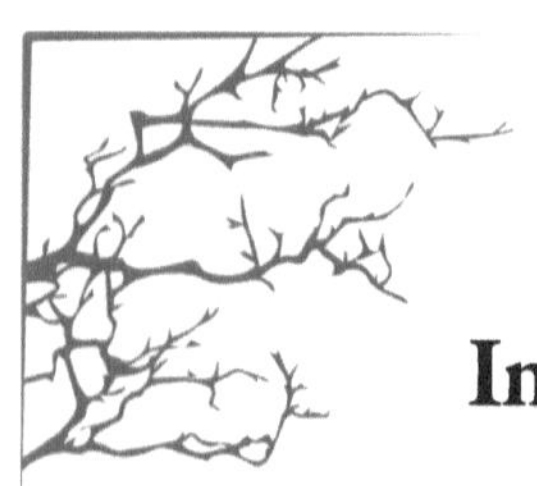

Into the Unknown

The days in Resurgam had been full of progress, the survivors strengthening their defenses and continuing the work of rebuilding. The walls stood tall now, their sturdy frame a symbol of their newfound strength. Watchtowers rose on each corner, offering a commanding view of the valley and the surrounding wilderness. But despite the safety they had found within their walls, Emmalyn knew that the battle was far from over. Resurgam was a sanctuary, yes—but it was not invincible.

It had been months since the Great Battle, and though the demons had retreated, Emmalyn could feel the weight of something darker on the horizon. The Great Tribulation was not finished. They could not remain complacent, content to simply rebuild. If they were to survive, they needed to know what lay beyond the safety of their walls.

"Scouting parties," Emmalyn said one evening as she stood before the gathered survivors, her voice firm and resolute. "We need to send out teams to scout the surrounding areas. We can't wait for the next attack to come to us. We need to know what's out there, what's changed, and who might still need help."

The group fell into quiet contemplation. They had made a home here, but Emmalyn's words reminded them that their peace was tenuous. The world outside was still dangerous.

"I'll go," Noah said, standing up from where he had been sitting with Caitlyn. Despite his injuries, his voice was steady. "I can't just sit here while the rest of you prepare. We need information, and I'm ready to help get it."

"Me too," Caitlyn added, stepping forward beside Noah. "We're a team, and we've faced worse than this."

Emmalyn nodded at them both. "It's important we move quickly and stay quiet. These scouting missions are not about confrontation—they're about gathering information. The more we know about the world around us, the better prepared we'll be. We leave in groups of three, and you'll be back before nightfall. We're not going too far from the town, but we need to know what threats are out there."

"I'll lead one of the groups," Colt volunteered. "I know the terrain, and I'm good at staying out of sight. I'll make sure we don't run into trouble."

"I'll take a group to the north," Kelli said. "We've been hearing strange things from that direction, and I think it's worth checking out."

Emmalyn stood in front of them, feeling the weight of the decision in her heart. She had led them through so much, but this felt different—sending out parties into the unknown, knowing they might find dangers they weren't prepared for.

"No matter what you find, return before dusk," she instructed. "We can't afford to let ourselves be caught off guard. Keep your weapons sharp and your eyes open. Report back immediately if you see anything unusual."

The teams prepared in silence, gathering their supplies—water, food, weapons, and a few tools that might be useful for communication or survival. Emmalyn watched them, her heart heavy with a mixture of pride and apprehension. She trusted them all, but this wasn't a simple scouting mission. This was the beginning of a journey into a world that might be even more dangerous than they imagined.

The first team set out early in the morning, the sky still dark with the remnants of night. Noah, Caitlyn, and Colt moved out quietly, following the worn trail that led into the dense forest. The trees here were ancient, their towering trunks casting long shadows over the ground as they moved in silence.

"We stick together," Colt said, his voice low and steady. "Eyes wide. This isn't just a walk in the woods. If we encounter anything, we act fast. Don't take unnecessary risks."

Noah nodded, though his thoughts were already drifting to what lay ahead. He hadn't fully healed from the injuries he had sustained months ago, but his sense of duty was stronger than ever. He couldn't sit idle in Resurgam while the world remained uncertain.

"We're ready," Caitlyn whispered. "We know what to do."

They moved swiftly through the trees, the morning light just beginning to filter through the canopy. The forest was quiet, save for the occasional rustle of leaves or distant birdcall. It was peaceful—but they all knew the peace was temporary. The deeper they went, the more they became aware of the vast emptiness around them.

Hours passed as they scouted the area, marking landmarks and checking for signs of movement. The further they went, the more the landscape shifted. Trees grew thicker, the underbrush more tangled, and the air seemed to grow heavier.

"I don't like this," Colt muttered as they approached a clearing. "It's too quiet."

Noah scanned the area, his hand instinctively moving to his sword. "Stay alert. This doesn't feel right."

Suddenly, a rustling sound broke the silence, followed by a sharp growl. The three of them instinctively pulled together, their weapons raised. Through the trees, a large figure emerged—a creature they hadn't seen before. It was a massive, hulking beast, covered in matted fur, with glowing yellow eyes. Its sharp teeth glinted in the sunlight as it snarled at them, its claws digging into the earth.

Without thinking, Colt drew his sword, his voice calm but commanding. "Get back. Stay in formation."

Caitlyn stepped forward, spear in hand, ready to defend the group. "What is that thing?"

Noah tightened his grip on his sword, his heart racing. "I don't know, but it's not friendly."

The beast charged, its massive form barreling toward them with surprising speed. The three of them scattered, moving quickly to avoid its attack. Caitlyn thrust her spear forward, aiming for the beast's exposed side. It howled in pain but didn't relent, turning toward her with furious speed.

"Noah, Caitlyn, fall back!" Colt ordered as he engaged the beast, his sword clashing with its claws. The sound was deafening, like metal on stone.

They worked as a unit, Noah and Caitlyn darting in to strike when the creature was distracted. It was a fierce battle, the beast relentless in its attack, but they managed to wound it—Caitlyn's spear punctured its flank, and Noah's sword cut deep into its shoulder.

The creature staggered, letting out a final, horrific roar before it collapsed, dead on the ground. The survivors stood over it, their chests heaving as adrenaline coursed through their veins.

"That... was close," Caitlyn breathed, wiping the sweat from her brow.

"I told you," Colt said, still catching his breath. "This is why we don't go too far alone. There's danger out there, more than we know."

Noah nodded, his hand still trembling slightly on the hilt of his sword. "We need to report this back to Emmalyn. She'll need to know about these creatures."

The team quickly made their way back toward Resurgam, the tension of the battle still lingering in their minds. They had faced something new, something the land had been hiding. Whatever lay ahead, they knew they weren't just fighting demons—they were fighting a world that had changed, that was still full of threats and dangers they hadn't yet understood.

As the sun began to dip below the horizon, they finally reached the gates of Resurgam, their minds full of the discovery they had made.

"No matter how much we fortify this place, the danger is still out there," Colt said, looking over his shoulder at the distant woods.

Emmalyn greeted them at the gates, her face full of concern and anticipation. "What did you find?"

Noah didn't hesitate. "Creatures. Large, dangerous, and aggressive. We don't know what they are, but we've never seen anything like them before."

Emmalyn's face grew serious. "Then we need to prepare for more than just demons. We need to be ready for anything."

The survivors gathered, ready to report their findings. The scouting mission had confirmed one thing—Resurgam was not just a sanctuary. It was a battleground, and the enemy was more varied and dangerous than they had anticipated.

But they would face it together. They had no choice. And together, they would rise.

The Shadows of Power

The survivors returned to Resurgam with the news of Roland Harris and his broadcast. The air was thick with the weight of what they had discovered. Emmalyn gathered the group together in the newly built church, its walls strong and sturdy, a symbol of their faith and their unity. The floorboards creaked beneath the survivors' boots, and the glow from the lanterns flickered in the dim light as everyone assembled, eager for answers.

The small crowd fell silent as Emmalyn stepped forward, her face set with determination. She shared the details of what they had found, speaking of Roland Harris's message, his broadcast of a new world government, and the sense of urgency in his voice.

"He's building something," Emmalyn said, her voice steady but concerned. "Something bigger than just a group of survivors. He's reaching out to others, trying to unite what's left of the world. But there's more to this—there's something unsettling about it. A new government? A world order? We need to be cautious. We need to know what we're getting into before we even think about contacting him or joining forces."

The survivors murmured among themselves, their concerns echoing through the room. They had worked so hard to rebuild, to find peace in Resurgam, and now this unknown figure, this Roland Harris, had come into their lives, offering promises of a new world.

Wheels, who had been quietly listening from his spot near the back, cleared his throat. His expression was serious, his brow furrowed as though piecing together something crucial. "Emmalyn's right to be cautious. But I've been thinking—something about this doesn't sit right with me."

The room quieted as everyone turned to look at Wheels. His weathered face was more lined than ever, his experience in the world before the Fall giving him a unique understanding of power and the ways people manipulated it.

"You're thinking what I'm thinking, right?" Noah asked, his voice tinged with suspicion.

Wheels nodded slowly. "I'm thinking that Roland Harris, and the government he's trying to build, might be something far darker than we realize. This isn't just about survival. It's about control. And control like that often comes at a terrible cost."

The room fell into silence again, the weight of Wheels' words heavy in the air. Emmalyn stepped forward, her voice steady but filled with concern. "What do you mean, Wheels?"

Wheels stood up, his mind clearly racing. "I've seen this before. A man with a vision. A man promising safety, unity, and a new world. But it's all about power. And those kinds of leaders—they rarely lead to anything good. I'm not sure Roland Harris is the man he claims to be. In fact... I'm starting to wonder if we're looking at someone far more dangerous."

"Dangerous?" Kelli asked, her voice sharp. "You think he's a threat?"

Wheels looked each of them in the eye before speaking. "What if Roland Harris is connected to something bigger—something far darker? Something the Bible warns us about. A leader who rises to power in the final days, a leader who promises peace but brings destruction. The Anti-Christ."

The room went still at the mention of the name. Annabeth's eyes widened, and even Emmalyn's heart skipped a beat. The weight of Wheels' words hung heavily in the air.

"You're saying Roland Harris could be the Anti-Christ?" Emmalyn asked, disbelief and concern mingling in her voice.

Wheels took a breath, his face grim. "I'm not saying he is, not yet. But think about it. The Anti-Christ is supposed to be a charismatic leader, someone who rises to power during the Tribulation, uniting people under false promises of peace, prosperity, and salvation. Roland Harris is doing exactly that. He's speaking about reuniting the world, building a new government, offering a solution to the chaos that's plagued humanity. He's gathering people to follow him, promising a future where everyone can thrive under his rule."

"But we don't know if he's really trying to deceive people," Kelli argued, her tone uncertain. "He could just be trying to help. He's trying to unite survivors, give them hope. Isn't that what we're doing?"

Wheels shook his head slowly. "It's not just about the promises, Kelli. The Anti-Christ's power isn't only about his words—it's about his control. He doesn't just want to unite people. He wants to control them. And the closer they get to him, the more they give up their freedom. He will manipulate, deceive, and lead them to believe they are safe—when in reality, they're walking into a trap."

Noah leaned forward, his face thoughtful. "But how does that tie into Roland? He's just a man, right? He can't be... the Anti-Christ."

"Roland doesn't have to be the Anti-Christ himself," Wheels continued, "but he could be the one setting the stage for his arrival. There are signs—the way people like Roland gather followers, the way they manipulate fear and desperation to get others to join them. They promise safety, stability, and peace, but their true goal is control, dominance, and destruction. I've seen it before. First with the false leaders of the world that fell, and now—if we're not careful—again with Roland."

Emmalyn felt a chill creep up her spine. The more she thought about it, the more Wheels' words made sense. Roland Harris's call for a new world government, his promise of unity—could it be that his motives were far more sinister than they appeared?

"We need to be cautious," Emmalyn said, her voice clear and firm. "We'll keep gathering information. We need to know exactly what he's doing, who he's really working with, and what his true goals are. But we can't afford to trust him blindly. Not without knowing more."

"We'll send another scouting party," Kelli suggested. "Maybe we can find out who else is involved. If Roland really is building something dangerous, we need to stop it before it spreads."

Wheels nodded. "Exactly. We don't know if Roland Harris is directly connected to the Anti-Christ, but we can't ignore the possibility. We must prepare for the worst—because if this is what we think it is, the peace we've fought for here in Resurgam could be the calm before the storm."

The survivors stood in solemn silence, the weight of Wheels' words heavy in the air. They had built Resurgam from the ground up, creating a sanctuary for themselves and others. But now, as they faced the possibility of a new threat—one that could reshape the world—they knew they had to be ready. They couldn't let the dangers of the past repeat themselves. They had to stay vigilant, protect their home, and prepare for whatever would come next.

Emmalyn looked around at her friends, at the people she had come to call family. Their bond was strong, their resolve unshakable. Together, they would face whatever the future held—and if Roland Harris truly was the harbinger of something darker, they would fight to protect the future they had fought so hard to create.

The battle for Resurgam was far from over. But as long as they stood together, with their faith and their strength, they would rise against any darkness that threatened their world.

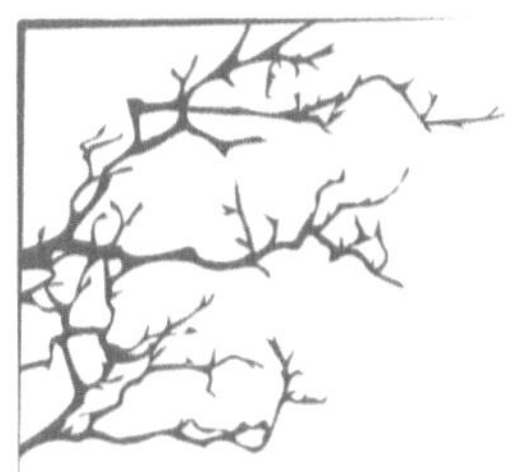

Tuning In

The decision to send out another scouting party came swiftly after Wheels' warning. The urgency of learning more about Roland Harris and his supposed new world government outweighed the risks. If he was truly a threat—or connected to an even greater one—they needed to know.

Noah, Caitlyn, and Colt volunteered to lead the mission, along with Clara. Their objective was clear: locate and acquire a functioning long-range radio so Resurgam could monitor Roland's broadcasts. The old radio frequencies could provide invaluable insight into his plans, his allies, and his base of operations.

"Stay sharp," Emmalyn said as they prepared to leave. "The last scouting mission proved the world out there isn't as empty as it seems. Whatever you find, get back here safely. We'll be waiting."

The group nodded in unison, their determination evident. With supplies packed and weapons ready, they set out at dawn, heading toward a region they'd only explored briefly during earlier missions. The journey was long, the terrain rugged and unforgiving, but their purpose kept them moving forward.

By midday, the group stumbled upon an old military outpost, its once-proud walls now overrun by vines and debris. The faded insignia on the gate suggested it had belonged to a pre-collapse communications hub—a promising lead.

"This looks like the place," Noah said, scanning the perimeter. "If there's a radio anywhere, it'll be here."

"Let's move carefully," Colt added, motioning for the group to spread out. "No telling what—or who—might still be inside."

The survivors entered the outpost cautiously, their footsteps echoing in the empty halls. The air was stale, the remnants of paper maps and broken equipment scattered across the floors. Despite the decay, the building's layout suggested it had once been a hub of activity.

"It's eerie," Caitlyn murmured, her spear at the ready. "Like the ghosts of the old world are still here."

"Let's hope the ghosts left something useful behind," Clara said, her tone grim but focused.

In the control room, they found what they were looking for: a dusty but intact long-range radio. It was mounted on a desk surrounded by rusted dials and switches. Though its exterior was weathered, the equipment appeared functional.

"This is it," Noah said, brushing off the dust and inspecting the machine. "If we can get this working, we'll be able to listen to Roland's broadcasts directly."

"Think it still works?" Caitlyn asked, eyeing the device skeptically.

"We'll make it work," Colt said, his voice steady. "Help me gather anything that looks like it might power this thing."

The group scavenged the room, finding batteries, spare parts, and a small portable generator tucked away in a storage closet. After some careful tinkering, the radio crackled to life, its signal faint but unmistakable.

"Let's test it," Noah said, adjusting the dials. The static faded, replaced by the clear voice of Roland Harris.

"This is Roland Harris, broadcasting to all survivors on the old emergency frequency. If you can hear this, know that you are not alone. We are rebuilding. We are creating a new future—a future where humanity can rise again, stronger than before. Join us in Old Amman, Jordan, where the foundations of this new world are being laid. Together, we can restore what was lost. Together, we can build something greater."

The group exchanged uneasy glances as Roland's voice filled the room. His tone was confident, charismatic, almost soothing. But beneath the surface, there was something unsettling—an undertone of authority that demanded obedience.

"Old Amman?" Clara said, frowning. "That city fell years ago. It's a ruin. Why would he set up there?"

"Strategic location, maybe," Colt speculated. "Amman's geography makes it defensible, and if he's using old tech, it might've been one of the last places with working infrastructure."

Caitlyn's brow furrowed. "It doesn't feel right. Why go to all this effort to rebuild in a place that's so broken? Unless..."

"Unless he wants the symbolism," Noah finished grimly. "Rising from the ashes of a fallen city. It's a statement—showing the world he's bringing order out of chaos."

Roland's broadcast continued, the cadence of his words almost hypnotic. "In this new world, there is no division. No fear. Only unity. Only strength. Join us, and together, we will reclaim humanity's destiny."

The static returned as the broadcast ended, leaving the room in silence.

"This changes things," Noah said, his voice low. "He's not just talking about survival. He's talking about control. He's setting himself up as the one person everyone should follow. That's more than just rebuilding. That's a power grab."

"Exactly what Wheels was warning us about," Caitlyn added, her expression dark. "This isn't just about restoring order. It's about creating his own version of it."

Colt crossed his arms, his gaze fixed on the radio. "Old Amman. If he's setting up there, he's got resources. Protection. People. And he's broadcasting like this—he's reaching a lot more survivors than just us. If we're not careful, we'll be walking straight into his trap."

Clara nodded, her voice quiet but firm. "But we need to know more. If he's really connected to what Wheels was talking about—the Anti-Christ, the Tribulation—then we can't ignore this."

"We won't ignore it," Noah said. "But we won't rush into anything either. We take this radio back to Resurgam. We listen. We learn. And then we decide what to do."

The group packed the radio and its parts carefully, ensuring everything was secure for the journey back. As they left the outpost, their minds were heavy with the knowledge they now carried. Roland Harris wasn't just a name. He was a force—a presence reaching across the broken world, calling survivors to his cause.

Whether he was a savior or a danger remained to be seen. But one thing was certain: Resurgam had to be ready.

When the group returned to Resurgam, the radio in tow, they were met with a mix of relief and curiosity. Emmalyn, Wheels, and the others listened intently as Noah recounted what they had discovered, his voice steady but tinged with urgency.

"Old Amman," Wheels murmured, his expression dark. "A city that fell, now rising again under the leadership of one man. If this isn't a warning sign, I don't know what is."

"We have the radio now," Noah said. "We can listen to his broadcasts, figure out what he's planning. But we need to be careful. This isn't just a call for unity. It's a call for power."

Emmalyn nodded, her resolve firm. "We'll monitor the broadcasts. We'll prepare. And we'll decide when and how to act. But one thing is clear—we can't let Roland Harris go unchecked. If he's a threat to this world, to everything we're rebuilding, then we have to stop him."

The survivors agreed, their determination growing stronger. Resurgam was no longer just a sanctuary. It was becoming a beacon of resistance, a place where they would fight to protect the truth and the hope they had built.

As the radio crackled to life again, Roland's voice filled the room once more, his words weaving promises of a brighter future. But in Resurgam, the survivors knew better than to trust blindly.

They would listen. They would learn. And they would stand ready. For whatever came next.

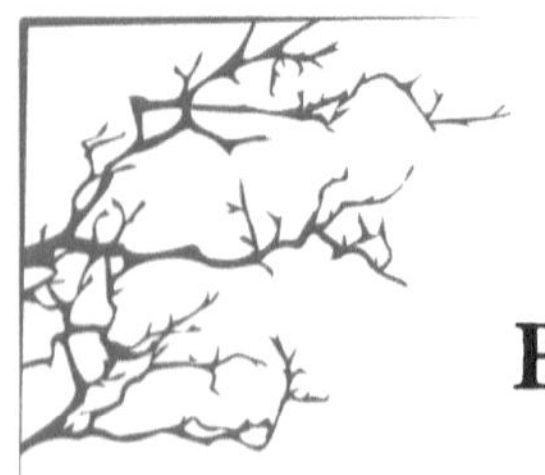

Eyes on Amman

The atmosphere in Resurgam was tense as the survivors gathered in the church to discuss their next move. The radio sat at the front of the room, its faint hum a reminder of the broadcasts that had sparked this meeting. Roland Harris's voice had filled the room just hours before, his promises of unity and a new world order raising as many questions as concerns.

Wheels stood near the pulpit, his face solemn. "We've heard enough to know that Roland Harris is dangerous. He's not just rebuilding. He's consolidating power. And if we wait too long, he might grow too strong for anyone to stop."

Emmalyn nodded, her arms crossed. "We've prepared for threats before, but this isn't just another demon or wild beast. This is a man with influence, resources, and a vision for the world. If he's as dangerous as we think, we need to see it for ourselves."

The room murmured in agreement, but there was hesitation in some of their faces.

"We've worked hard to make Resurgam safe," Kelli said, her voice steady but uncertain. "Do we really want to risk everything by going out there? What if we bring back more trouble than we can handle?"

"We can't ignore this," Noah said, his tone resolute. "If we sit here and do nothing, we'll be blindsided when his reach extends to us. We need to understand what we're up against."

Caitlyn stepped forward, standing beside Noah. "He's not just talking to survivors. He's building something bigger, something that could affect all of us. The only way to know the truth is to see it for ourselves."

Wheels gestured toward the radio. "Roland mentioned Old Amman, a city that's been in ruins for years. If he's using it as his base, there's a reason. Strategic location, symbolism, resources—we need to know why he chose that place and what he's doing there."

Colt leaned against the wall, arms crossed. "It's risky. We don't know what kind of security he has, what kind of people are working with him. But if we're careful, we might be able to get close enough to find out without being noticed."

Emmalyn turned to the group, her expression firm. "Then it's decided. We send a small team to Amman to investigate. The rest of us stay here and continue fortifying Resurgam. If we're walking into something dangerous, we need to be ready."

The discussion shifted to who would go. Emmalyn wanted to lead the team herself, but Wheels insisted she stay behind to lead the community in her absence.

"You're the heart of this place," Wheels said firmly. "If something happens to you, Resurgam loses more than just a leader. We need you here."

Reluctantly, Emmalyn agreed, but she chose the team with care. Noah and Caitlyn were selected for their resilience and experience. Colt's tactical mind and combat skills made him an obvious choice, and Clara volunteered to join as a scout, her sharp eyes and quiet movements invaluable for navigating the unknown.

"You'll need to travel light and stay out of sight," Emmalyn said as she briefed them. "Your goal is to observe, gather information, and get back safely. We're not engaging with anyone unless absolutely necessary."

Noah nodded. "We'll find out what's going on and bring back everything we can. You'll know exactly what we're dealing with."

The team prepared quickly, packing only what they needed—supplies, weapons, and a map of the region. They left before dawn the next morning, the rest of Resurgam watching as they disappeared into the horizon.

The road to Old Amman was long and treacherous, the landscape shifting from rolling hills to barren wastelands. The team moved cautiously, avoiding the remnants of collapsed cities and the creatures that roamed the wilderness.

As they drew closer to Amman, the air grew heavier, the signs of human activity becoming more apparent. Abandoned vehicles lined the roads, and makeshift camps dotted the outskirts of the ruined city.

"It's definitely not deserted," Caitlyn observed, her voice low.

Noah pointed to a distant hill where a figure stood silhouetted against the skyline. "They've got patrols. We're getting close."

The team moved to higher ground, finding a vantage point that overlooked the city. From their position, they could see the remnants of Old Amman—a sprawling urban ruin with crumbling buildings and overgrown streets. But amidst the decay, something new had emerged.

At the city's center, a massive compound had been constructed. High walls surrounded the area, and guard towers were positioned at every corner. The faint hum of machinery filled the air, and the glow of electric lights illuminated the compound even as the sun began to set.

"They've got power," Clara said, her voice tinged with disbelief. "That's not just some survivor camp. That's a fortress."

Colt nodded, his expression grim. "This isn't just rebuilding. This is militarization. Look at the guards—uniforms, weapons, patrol patterns. This isn't random."

The team stayed hidden, watching as people moved in and out of the compound. Some looked like civilians, weary and desperate, while others wore uniforms and carried rifles. Trucks laden with supplies rolled through the gates, and workers unloaded crates marked with strange symbols.

"What's in those crates?" Caitlyn wondered aloud.

"Something we don't want to be on the receiving end of," Colt replied.

Noah's gaze hardened as he watched the activity below. "This isn't just about uniting people. This is about control. Look at them—they're building an army."

The team continued to observe, documenting everything they could. They noted the guard rotations, the flow of supplies, and the structure of the compound. But as night fell, something unexpected happened.

The compound's courtyard filled with people as Roland Harris emerged onto a raised platform. The floodlights illuminated his face, his presence commanding. His voice echoed across the city as he addressed the crowd, his tone calm yet powerful.

"Brothers and sisters," Roland began, his arms outstretched. "Today marks another step toward the restoration of our world. Together, we are building a future free from chaos and fear. Here, in the heart of a fallen city, we are rising again. This is the beginning of a new era—an era of unity, strength, and prosperity."

The crowd erupted in applause, their cheers echoing through the ruined streets.

"We have been scattered, broken, and lost," Roland continued. "But no more. Under my leadership, we will reclaim what was taken from us. We will rebuild civilization, stronger and more resilient than ever before. And to those who doubt us, to those who resist this new order, know this: their time is over. The future belongs to us."

The team exchanged uneasy glances as Roland's voice carried on. His words were laced with promises of peace, but there was an underlying edge—a warning to anyone who stood in his way.

"This is bigger than we thought," Caitlyn whispered. "He's not just leading. He's taking over."

"We've seen enough," Colt said, his voice firm. "Let's get back to Resurgam. They need to hear this."

The team retreated under the cover of darkness, their minds racing with what they had witnessed. Roland Harris wasn't just building a government—he was building a regime.

As they made their way back to Resurgam, one thing was clear: the battle for the future had already begun. And Resurgam would need to decide where they stood in the fight.

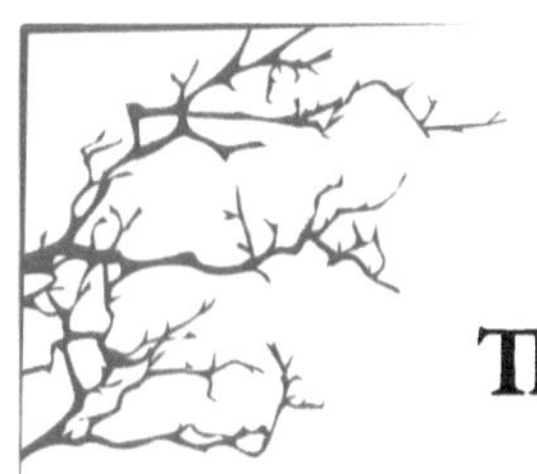

The Storm Breaks

The scouting team returned to Resurgam in the dead of night, their faces etched with urgency and exhaustion. Emmalyn met them at the gates, her heart sinking at the sight of their expressions. Whatever they had found in Old Amman had confirmed their worst fears.

"What did you see?" Emmalyn asked as they gathered in the church, the weight of their journey apparent in every movement.

Noah was the first to speak, his voice steady but grim. "Roland isn't just uniting people. He's creating an army. The compound in Old Amman—it's a fortress. He has weapons, guards, and more resources than we've ever seen. He's preparing for something big."

"And it's not just about rebuilding," Caitlyn added. "His speeches are filled with promises of unity and strength, but there's an edge to his words. He's not offering peace. He's demanding allegiance."

Colt leaned forward, his arms crossed. "He's preparing for war. And if we don't act soon, we'll be on the receiving end of whatever he's planning."

Wheels, sitting at the front of the room, nodded slowly. "This is it," he said, his voice filled with quiet certainty. "The final battle. We've seen the signs, heard the warnings. Roland Harris isn't just a man with ambition. He's the beginning of something far darker. This is the moment we've been preparing for."

The room fell silent as the weight of Wheels' words settled over the group. They had known this day would come, but the reality of it was more daunting than they had imagined.

"What do we do?" Annabeth asked, her voice trembling. "We can't just wait for him to come to us."

Emmalyn stood, her gaze sweeping over the survivors. "No, we can't. We've built this place to be a sanctuary, but it's also our stronghold. If Roland and his army come here, we'll be ready. But we can't just defend—we need to take the fight to him. We need to stand for what's right, for the people who can't stand for themselves."

Wheels nodded. "This isn't just about us. This is about the world. If Roland succeeds, his reign will bring suffering, control, and destruction. We have to stop him before he becomes unstoppable."

The survivors moved with purpose, their fear giving way to determination. The walls of Resurgam had been fortified for months, and now every trap, weapon, and defense would be put to the test.

Weapons were sharpened, arrows fletched, and shields reinforced. The church became a rallying point, its walls adorned with verses of courage and strength. Survivors gathered there to pray, their voices lifting in unison as Wheels led them in asking for guidance and protection.

"*Do not be afraid or discouraged because of this vast army,*" Wheels said, quoting from 2 Chronicles 20:15. "*For the battle is not yours, but God's.*"

The scouting team shared what they had learned about Roland's forces, detailing the weapons and tactics they had observed. Colt took charge of the battle plan, his tactical mind working tirelessly to anticipate the enemy's moves.

"We'll divide into groups," he explained, pointing to a map of Resurgam and its surrounding area. "One group will hold the walls, keeping them from breaching the town. Another will focus on their flanks, disrupting their lines and slowing their advance. And if it comes down to it, we'll fall back to the church. It's the strongest structure we have."

Noah and Caitlyn worked to organize the survivors, assigning roles and ensuring everyone knew their part. Even the youngest and weakest were given tasks—carrying supplies, tending to the wounded, or reinforcing the defenses.

"This is our home," Noah said, his voice filled with conviction. "And we're not giving it up without a fight."

At dawn, the first signs of Roland's army appeared on the horizon. The survivors watched from the walls as a column of soldiers marched toward Resurgam, their banners fluttering in the wind. The sun glinted off their weapons, and the ground seemed to tremble beneath their boots.

In the distance, a black armored vehicle rolled forward, its imposing presence a stark contrast to the rustic simplicity of Resurgam. Standing atop it was Roland Harris himself, his arms outstretched as he addressed his army.

"Today," Roland's voice boomed, amplified by speakers, "we bring order to chaos. We reclaim what was lost and unite this world under one banner. Those who stand against us stand against progress. Against hope. Against the future."

The survivors listened in silence, the weight of his words filling the air. But Emmalyn stepped forward, her voice cutting through the tension.

"He doesn't know us," she said, her gaze fierce. "He doesn't know what we've built here, what we've fought for. Resurgam isn't just a place. It's a promise. And we're going to show him that promise is worth fighting for."

As Roland's forces moved closer, the survivors took their positions. The walls were lined with archers, the gates reinforced with barricades, and the open fields littered with hidden traps.

The battle began with a deafening roar as Roland's army charged toward the walls. The survivors held their ground, arrows raining down on the advancing soldiers. Traps triggered, explosions ripping through the enemy's ranks as they stumbled over hidden mines and spiked pits.

Colt led the defenders at the gate, his sword flashing as he engaged the first wave of soldiers. "Hold the line!" he shouted, his voice cutting through the chaos. "Don't let them through!"

Caitlyn fought alongside him, her spear striking with precision as she pushed back the attackers. "They're relentless!" she called, her voice filled with both fear and determination.

"They're just men," Noah said, stepping in to block an attack. "We've faced worse."

Meanwhile, Clara and a small group of scouts flanked the enemy, striking from the shadows to disrupt their formations. Their hit-and-run tactics slowed the advance, buying precious time for the defenders.

From his position atop the armored vehicle, Roland watched the battle with cold calculation. "Send in the second wave," he ordered, his voice calm. "They're putting up a fight, but it won't last."

As the second wave advanced, Emmalyn led a group of reinforcements to the walls, rallying the survivors with her presence. "We've trained for this!" she shouted. "We've prepared! Remember what we're fighting for!"

The defenders redoubled their efforts, their resolve unshaken despite the enemy's numbers. But as the battle raged on, a new sound filled the air—a deep, guttural roar that sent a chill through everyone on the battlefield.

From the ranks of Roland's army emerged a massive creature, its hulking form covered in jagged armor. Its eyes glowed with an unnatural light, and its claws tore through the ground as it charged toward the gates.

"What is that?" Caitlyn gasped, her grip tightening on her spear.

"A new kind of nightmare," Noah muttered, his eyes narrowing. "But we're not backing down."

As the creature barreled toward the gates, Emmalyn raised her sword, her voice steady despite the fear in her heart. "Together," she said, her gaze sweeping over the survivors. "We stand together."

The final battle for Resurgam had begun. And as the defenders prepared to face the darkness, they knew one thing for certain: they would fight with everything they had, not just for their lives, but for the hope that had brought them this far.

This was their home. And they would protect it—no matter the cost.

Defiance and Destiny

The battlefield was a cacophony of chaos. Roland's army surged against Resurgam's walls, their relentless assault pushing the defenders to their limits. The monstrous creature that led the second wave tore through traps and debris, its roars shaking the ground. But within the walls of Resurgam, resolve burned bright. The survivors were no strangers to battles for survival, and this was no different.

At the gates, Colt and Caitlyn fought side by side, their weapons flashing in the morning light. Clara and her scouts continued their hit-and-run attacks, targeting the enemy's weakest points. Above them, archers loosed arrows with unyielding precision, their aim steady despite the rising tension.

Near the church, Emmalyn rallied the defenders, her voice cutting through the din. "Hold the line! We've faced worse than this—we are stronger than they know!"

The monstrous creature slammed against the gates, its claws rending the wooden beams. Noah led a group to reinforce the barricade, planting spears and shields in its path to slow its advance.

"We need to bring it down!" Noah shouted, his voice hoarse from shouting orders.

"I'll distract it," Caitlyn called, gripping her spear tightly. "You take the shot!"

With unshakable courage, Caitlyn moved into the creature's path, her movements swift as she dodged its attacks. Her spear flashed, striking the beast's armored hide and drawing its attention. As it roared and turned toward her, Noah took his chance.

"Now!" he yelled.

Colt hurled a makeshift explosive—a small barrel filled with oil and nails—at the creature's exposed flank. The explosion rocked the battlefield, and the beast let out a final, guttural roar before collapsing in a heap.

The defenders cheered, but their victory was short-lived. Roland's voice echoed from his position atop the armored vehicle, amplified by speakers.

"You think you've won?" he called, his tone calm but laced with menace. "This is only the beginning. You can't stop progress. You can't stop destiny. Stand down now, and I may show mercy. Resist, and you'll face annihilation."

Emmalyn's gaze locked onto Roland, her heart pounding. She climbed to the top of the wall, her voice strong as she responded.

"This is our home!" she shouted, her words ringing out over the battlefield. "We don't bow to tyrants. You may have your army, your machines, and your power, but we have something stronger. We have each other, and we have faith. You'll never take Resurgam."

Roland's expression darkened, but before he could respond, the sound of retreating horns filled the air. His forces began to fall back, retreating beyond the hills. It wasn't a defeat, Emmalyn realized—it was a calculated withdrawal.

"This isn't over," Noah said, watching the enemy fade into the distance.

"No," Emmalyn agreed, her jaw set. "It's not."

The survivors gathered in the church that evening, their spirits bruised but unbroken. The air was thick with both relief and apprehension. They had won the day, but they all knew it was a temporary victory. Roland's army would regroup, and when they returned, they would be stronger, more prepared.

Wheels addressed the group, his voice steady despite the day's events. "Today, we stood against the darkness, and we pushed it back. But make no mistake—this was just the beginning. Roland Harris isn't finished. He'll come again, and next time, he'll bring everything he has. We must be ready."

Emmalyn stood beside him, her gaze sweeping over the survivors. "We've built something incredible here. A home. A sanctuary. And we've proven that we can protect it. But Roland isn't just a threat to us. He's a threat to everyone. We need to decide how far we're willing to go to stop him."

Colt crossed his arms, his expression thoughtful. "We need allies. If Roland is building an empire, we can't face him alone. There must be other groups out there—survivors like us—who are willing to fight back."

"Then we start reaching out," Caitlyn said, her voice filled with resolve. "We find others. We build a network. If Roland wants a war, we'll give him one—but on our terms."

Wheels nodded. "And we prepare. Spiritually, physically, emotionally. The battles ahead will test us in ways we can't imagine. But with faith, we will endure."

As the survivors dispersed to tend to their wounds and reinforce the town's defenses, Emmalyn found herself standing at the edge of the walls, looking out over the darkened horizon. Noah joined her, his arm in a makeshift sling but his spirit unbroken.

"We're still standing," he said quietly.

"For now," Emmalyn replied, her voice soft. "But we both know Roland isn't done. This was just the opening move."

Noah nodded, his gaze steady. "Then we keep fighting. Not just for Resurgam, but for everyone who's counting on us—even if they don't know it yet."

Emmalyn turned to him, her eyes reflecting a mix of determination and hope. "This isn't just about us anymore. Roland is playing a much bigger game. We're not just defending Resurgam—we're standing against everything he represents."

"And we're not alone," Noah added. "We'll find others. We'll build something stronger than anything he can tear down."

In the distance, the faint glow of Roland's retreating forces lingered on the horizon, a reminder of the battle that had been fought—and the war that was still to come.

As the first stars appeared in the night sky, Emmalyn whispered a silent prayer, her heart filled with both fear and resolve.

"Resurgam," she murmured. "We will rise again."

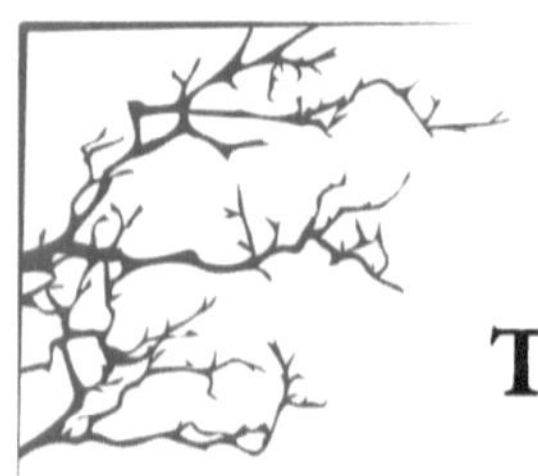

To Be Continued

The battle for Resurgam was far from over, but the survivors were ready. Together, they would face the challenges ahead, uniting their strength and their faith against the growing darkness.

The next chapter of their journey would take them beyond the walls of their sanctuary, into a world filled with danger, alliances, and the ultimate test of their resolve. The fight for the future had only just begun.